The Handfasters

The Handfasters

Helen Susan Swift

Published 2016 by Creativia
Paperback design by Creativia (www.creativia.org)
ISBN: 978-1530413706
Cover art by http://www.thecovercollection.com/

This book is dedicated to my Mum and to Cathy 'Mumski' Draper
With love

Contents

Prelude

Should I tell you?

Should I tell you everything?

Should I tell you everything that happened, or should I leave out the terrible secrets, the shared guilt and the intimacy and only mention the romance and the eventual outcome, how I came to be here and how everything was changed?

I am not sure what would be best.

If I write the whole story, you might think less of me, and wonder that somebody with my past can be in such a position, but on the other hand, if I only tell the good parts, you will know only the face of me that I allow the world to see. No: you are my blood; you deserve the truth, and nobody can alter what has already happened.

So I shall tell everything; every single detail, the good, the bad and the passionate, and then you may judge for yourself what kind of person I am. By the time you read this, all that will be left of me will be a memory whispering in the haunts of the hills, but maybe the autumn winds will carry the tune of my life. I hope so, for I have sung long and often here, the lifting songs of triumph, the soft sighs of love and the melancholic laments of loss.

You will never meet me, you girls and boys, but you may see my picture, hanging on the wall in its gilded frame. That is me, half way up the stairs, with my favourite blue dress trim around my hips and my hair as black as coal. It is dyed of course, for I am a lady of advanced age, and a grandmother and great grandmother and probably a great-great grandmother by now, knowing what sort of things you youngsters get up to. A lady of my age is entitled to grey hair, but I demand my vanity, and I will have it, and the raven hair that was my curse and my pride.

So I am watching you whenever you mount these stairs, and you may look on me after you read my words, and know what adventures and misadventures I had, and from what stock you come. And when you leave this house and walk in the surrounding hills you will take a little bit of me with you, in your heart and in your mind and in your soul, I hope.

For these are my hills, more than anybody else's, and here is my story. If you read it, you may perhaps not judge me too harshly. But remember always that I am part of you, so to condemn me is in great measure to condemn yourself.

Chapter One

I was a stranger to the wynds and closes of old Edinburgh, where the mists swirl around the tall stone tenements and the rain washes clean the cobbles in the morning. I did not know, then, that the ancient city claims a thousand secrets and nobody is ever what they seem at first. Call me naïve, if you will, but we are what life makes us and small blame to ourselves until we learn from bitter experience.

You may know Edinburgh, but nevertheless I will remind you about our Scottish capital. It is like nowhere else in the world, in my world at least, for it is a divided city, with Princes Street Gardens, the Nor' Loch that was, an oxymoron between two opposites. On one side sits the graceful squares and classical lines of the Georgian New Town, that most elegant of creations, where modern houses sit in grandly refined rows and people talk in quiet undertones. However, cross to the south side of the gardens and you enter the mediaeval hotchpotch of original Edinburgh, the Old Town of romance where queens once rubbed shoulders with commoners, devout ministers preached at unremitting blackguards and grand ladies exchanged bawdy wit with unlettered gutterbloods.

"This must be the most romantic city in the world," I said that December day in 1811 as I stared at the serrated skyline of the Old Town.

Louise laughed out loud, rather rudely, I thought, but I immediately forgave her when she favoured me with her smile. Everybody always forgave Louise, for she had such a winning way about her.

"Romance is what romance does," she said cryptically and tapped her ivory fan against my leg. "But what do you understand of romance, Alison Lamont?" Her eyes mocked me, their brilliant blue as beautiful as an angel's kiss and as innocent as the devil's tail.

I said nothing, for she had touched a sore spot in my life. I knew nothing of romance, or of much else, really, although I could speak fluent French, sew perfectly and paint as well as any young woman of eighteen. Only two years older than I, my cousin Louise, the beautiful, sophisticated Miss Ballantyne, had more experience in her little finger than I had in my whole body, and did she not know it?

Louise smiled again, displaying the perfect teeth that were her pride. "Don't you worry, Alison," she advised. "I'll soon introduce you to the ways of romance. A few weeks with me and you will be flirting with the best of them and teasing the most amiable men to the point of distraction." Opening her fan, she half hid her face behind it and peeped lopsidedly at me. "We'll take this city by its clacking heels,' she said, 'and shake loose the gaiety it tries to deny."

We were sitting side by side in Aunt Elspeth's coach at that time, jolting along Princes Street with the fine new houses rising to our left and the castle standing a grim sentinel over the murky waters of the Nor' Loch on our right.

"Now there's a sight to take the edge from a bright day," Louise was stretching across me, balancing with one hand on my knee as she peered outside.

I looked over, first at the castle, and then at the loch, which had what I took to be a burning boat on it. "That boat's on fire," I said, and Louise gave a disparaging little laugh and tapped me again with her fan.

"Indeed it is," she told me, "for there is a strange creature down there that sends boats out to the water and then burns them."

I understood strange creatures, for I had been reared on stories of water kelpies and uruisgs and fairy dogs but I had never heard of anything that burns boats before. I stared out of the window, expecting to see a horned monster at the side of the loch, but instead, there was only a tall and rather dishevelled man.

4

"There's no creature there," I was vaguely disappointed at the sight.

"That's Willie Kemp," Louise said, hiding her giggle behind her fan. "He's the strangest creature that ever was. They say that he does not talk to women, or to anybody else, but spends all his time making strange machines that don't work."

"Oh!" I looked away again, for I had no interest in a man who made strange machines. And why should I have had, when there were the delights of Edinburgh before me, and Lady Catriona's ball that very evening?'

"Does he not amuse you?" Louise was still staring out of the window, obviously amused at the antics of this Willie Kemp. "He is *such* a strange creature." Lowering her voice, as if we were in a crowded room rather than alone in Lady Elspeth's carriage, she bent close to my ear. "Do you know what some people say about him?"

I shook my head, "no," I said, for I was indeed very naive in those days. "What do they say?"

Louise told me, in deliberate and terrible detail, stories that would scandalise me even now, yet alone then, and I am sure that I was as red as any summer apple by the time that she was finished.

"Oh," I said, as Louise widened her eyes at the expression on my face.

"Oh my dear Alison," she said, placing a reassuring hand on my arm. "I hope that I have not shocked you."

"Not at all," I lied, wishing desperately for a corner in which to hide. I was an innocent in most matters, apart from the most basic.

"That's all serene then," Louise sank back in her seat, her eyes still amused. "But it's best to know these things, don't you see? And better for you to hear from me, who loves you as if you were the dearest of sisters, rather than from some stranger who does not have your best interests in her heart."

"Of course Louise," I forgave her at once, for she was always thinking about others, was Louise. "Will it be long before we arrive at the ball?"

"It will be no time at all. We just have to ascend the Earthen Mound and we'll be nearly there. The Forres Residence is about half way up the Castlehill."

I had heard of the Earthen Mound, that great accumulation of dirt and rubble from the building of the New Town that the thrifty burghers of Edinburgh had utilised as a bridge-cum-road to take them to the Old, but I had never seen it before. The coachman made the most of the incline, whistling and yelling to the poor horses in the coarsest possible manner as he drove up the ugly curve.

"Oh I do hate this part," Louise held on to her hat as if the angle of the coach would remove it from her undeniably pretty head.

I sighed and tried to look as composed as I knew how; I had not so quickly forgotten her scandalous stories. Opening my fan, I stirred the air in what I hoped was a languid fashion. "It is a trifle tiresome," I agreed, "but can hardly be compared to the *mountains* we have in Badenoch." I let her think of that for a while as I watched the view alter. The New Town looked even more impressive from here, with the grey squares so regular against the drab green of the winter countryside.

The Old Town, however, was less pleasant and much less romantic at close quarters than it had seemed from a distance. I do not know what I had expected, knights in armour, perhaps, and gay cavaliers on prancing horses, but instead we entered a long, sloping street that seemed like a ditch stuck between high cliff-like tenements, or lands as the gutterbloods of Edinburgh term them. Where I had expected romantic heroes, instead the streets were populated with ragamuffins in various attires, from Highland plaid that made me quite homesick to ragged breeches and torn shirts that would have disgraced a scarecrow on any Speyside field and were often quite short of decency.

"Welcome to the High Street," Louise seemed not to mind the pell-mell of people. "We'll be leaving the coach soon." Her eyes were as bright as I had ever seen them, shining with anticipation as she readied herself for the ball.

The coachman stopped at the entrance to what appeared to be a back alley, but which I was assured was the entrance to a wynd, one of the side streets that delved at right angles from the main road to the unseen heart of the old city. Rather than walk, Louise sent the man ahead, and he returned a minute later with two burly fellows carrying a sedan chair. I had never seen the like before, but Louise assured me that their use was normal amongst civilised people, and she slipped herself in with a great rustle of satin and a hint of exposed ankle that captured the porter's attention but must surely have been a mistake.

Now, I am aware that such vehicles are not common in this modern age, and so for the benefit of those of you who have never seen one, I shall describe a sedan. They were not large, being little more than a box big enough to hold a seated lady, with curtained windows at the sides and two long poles protruding at either end. One man lifted the poles at the front, another took the poles at the rear, they lifted the weight and walked away, carrying their passenger with a degree of comfort and as much privacy as drawn curtains would allow.

Unfortunately, there was but the one sedan, and two of us, which meant that I had to walk a few steps behind, just like a common servant. So my introduction to Edinburgh saw me following the chairmen as they slithered down the greasy cobbles of the wynd; a fine welcome to the Capital city, you will agree, but worse was to come, by-and-by.

I had no idea how malodorous an Edinburgh wynd could be, but that short walk was a revelation. I seemed to be walking into the very bowels of the earth, with the buildings looming so tall on either side that they blocked out what light December allowed, while the ground was an abode of every kind of filth imaginable. Well, I admit that I was young, but even so, I was disgusted by the stench, and I envied Louise her carriage, vowing never to walk abroad in the older part of Edinburgh again.

And then we stopped at what only be described as a gap in the cliff-like wall of the building. I had expected the entrance to Her Ladyship's dwelling to be something grand, with great sweeping stairs and liveried footmen on hand, but instead, it was a poky little hole in a projecting circular tower. The only saving grace was the carved coat armorial above the massive and studded door. That was indeed impressive, being of solid stone and was obviously ancient, with Her Ladyship's coat of arms as permanent as Scotland herself.

"Take me right inside," Louise ordered, as the chairmen halted outside the door, and the poor fellows, huffing with exertion, had to lift the whole contraption again and manoeuvre it through the doorway.

Once inside, all my preconceptions were removed. That short walk down the stinking wynd had prepared me for a vile, wretched abode of dark rooms, but the reality could not have been more different. As Louise extricated herself from the chair in a great flurry of satin, silks, skirts and artfully revealed petticoats, I stepped from the stone lobby past a spiral staircase and right into the most amazing room that I had ever seen. Sir Walter Scott himself could not have conceived of anything so delightful, with a massive oaken wainscot, a portrait, by Norrie, I fancied, although it might have been Raeburn, glowering moodily down and a fireplace so large that half a herd of cattle could have been roasted there. There was a long oval table so heavily polished that it could have reflected my face and a whole regiment of padded chairs standing at attention round about. It was like something from the court of King Arthur, except lit by a slowly swaying chandelier and presided over by two of the most delightful figures it had ever been my pleasure to behold.

One was simply the most elegant of elderly ladies imaginable. She must have been eighty if she was a day, and she wore the wide skirt and low neckline of fashionable France in her youth. She could have stepped straight from a picture of the court of King George, except for the great green turban on her head and the ivory fan that she languidly wafted in front of a face that was white with powder and enhanced by dark beauty spots. I dropped in a fine curtsey, for only a truly great lady could dress with so much style, and she acknowledged me with a gracious nod of her head.

"Young lady."

Her companion was tall, with a long green travelling cloak and a shiny tall hat of black beaver that he doffed as soon as I stepped inside the room. He made an elegant leg, but the effect was somewhat spoiled as he had to grab for his hat, which topped dangerously from his head and nearly landed on the floor at my feet.

"Miss Ballantyne?" He said when he straightened up, speaking in a soft accent with a strange drawl the like of which I had never heard before.

"No sir," I corrected gently. "Miss Ballantyne is my cousin. I am Alison Lamont."

"Ah." The gentleman belatedly doffed his so-lately-clutched-at hat, which sent his wig askew and allowed a quiff of auburn hair to flop forward over a face that was too tanned to be fashionable but still appeared most agreeable.

I stared at that face, wondering what sort of man could possess it. Although it had the features of a stranger, it possessed such amiability that I could not help but smile. His eyes were as green as a mountain lochan, and his nose as Highland as peat, long and straight and imposing.

"Alexander Forres," he introduced himself. "And this is my mother, Lady Catriona Forres, of Forres House and the Forres Residence."

I curtseyed again, to which he made a much more successful bow.

Louise entered then, hurrying in with one hand holding up her skirts and the other clutching her fan as if it were a weapon of war rather than a folding sliver of carved ivory.

"Then you are Miss Louise Ballantyne," Alexander Forres made the correct deduction, bowing once again.

Louise dropped in her most elegant curtsey, deliberately displaying her far-too-impressive cleavage to the eyes of Forres, who looked away as a true gentleman should. I liked him immediately and vowed that if I should ever be fortunate enough to find a suitor, he should be of the same calibre and possess the same fine manners as the honourable Alexander, although he would have to be considerably younger.

"Well now," Lady Catriona spoke for the first time, and everybody in that room paused to listen. "Now that we all know each other, perhaps we can repair upstairs, for I am sure that there will be no dancing in this room."

We followed her, of course, and you never saw so many butterflies and beaus before, for others had followed Louise and me so that great room was already overflowing with fluttering women and preening men. Ignoring any pretence at delicacy, Lady Catriona floated up a turnpike stair, with her wide skirt rubbing on both sides at once and her yellow high heeled shoes clicking and clacking on the bare stone beneath. Where Lady Catriona led, we must of necessity follow, and as she made no complaints about the starkness of her surroundings, why, then neither could we. All the same, I was surprised at the lack of decoration in that turnpike and the old fashioned torches that illuminated our passage. There was nothing modish at all, to be sure.

We hesitated outside a varnished door on which some long-gone master craftsman had carved the Forres crest, and through which floated the sounds of revelry and music. I took an audibly deep breath.

"Whatever are you doing?" Louise enquired, and I informed her that it was most fashionable to have colour on one's face before entering a ball.

"But not like that," Louise said and pinched her cheeks so the flush arose.

I copied her, but with more timidity so my face retained its creamy complexion.

"Oh, my," Louise said with a disapproving shake of her head. Removing her right glove, she gave me a resounding slap on my left cheek. "There now," she said with satisfaction and repeated the procedure with great energy on the other side. "That's much better."

Too astonished to scream, I could only stare as Lady Catriona nodded her approval.

"We all must suffer for fashion, must me not? That was a very sisterly thing to do, Miss Ballantyne."

With my face burning and without bothering to thank Louise for her kindness, I followed directly behind Lady Catriona as she pushed open her own door and swept into the upstairs room.

I did not step far in, for I had to stop and stare. The upstairs room was vast. It must have extended the entire length of the house, with an elaborately plastered ceiling and an array of windows that stretched along two entire walls. Crystal chandeliers splintered their light onto panelled walls, while a fire of near mediaeval proportions was bright in the fireplace.

All these details, of course, mattered nought compared to the company, and here Lady Catriona's guests excelled anything that I had seen before, and most that I have seen since. I mentioned the butterflies and beaus on the turnpike, but they were only a shadow of what waited in that upper room. I may have seen the cream of the company in Badenoch, but until that evening I was a baby in sophisticated company.

My first impression was of scarlet and feathers, with the occasional military kilt and sporran thrown in. I grew up deep in the heart of the Highlands, but I had never seen kilts like them before and the sight made me stifle an unladylike and very impolite giggle. Wherever did they get their ideas about Highland dress? I must have gaped at the tall feather bonnets and over-elaborate sporrans, the pointless plaids and cairngorm-decorated dirks that were about as Highland as they were Chinese, but I was also awed by the overall sense of splendour.

Nevertheless, I did think that the wearers of these exotic costumes more than made up for their strange appearance. To a man they were tall while those who were not young and handsome were dignified and imposing and all were military enough to frighten Bonaparte. I could feel Louise drawing herself taller, even as she arched her back and put on her most imperious expression.

"My, my," she said softly, "what a delicious display of officers. Now you follow my lead, young Alison, and we can find a fine husband for you."

"Husband?" I said, or rather squawked, for I am sure that my voice rose a score of octaves, "I did not come here for a husband!"

Louise's look was a mixture of astonishment and amusement, and once again she wielded that fan of hers, closing it and poking it sharply against my arm. "You did not come here for a husband? My dear, dear cousin Alison, pray tell me for what other reason you would possibly attend Lady Catriona's ball?"

I could not answer that I was only here for the dancing and because Aunt Elspeth had decided that I should go, so I gaped at her with my mouth open instead.

"Exactly so," Louise chose to take my silence for agreement. "So let us dance."

And so we did.

I have danced in many fine places since, but I will always remember that night as we bid a fond farewell to 1811 and welcomed the infant 1812. And what a year it was to prove, but of course we did not yet know that as we pirouetted and bowed and whirled away the night in a riot of bright colours and flashing shoulders and swirling kilts.

"You dance uncommonly well, miss … miss … I am sorry, but I do not know your name?"

My companion of the moment was as tall as any guardsman, with dark hair fashionably ruffled and a scarlet tunic that did nothing to conceal white breeches so tight they could have nearly have been painted in place.

"Nor I yours, sir, for we have not yet been formally introduced," I said, somewhat stiffly, for I was unused to such forward behaviour from a man posing as an officer and gentleman.

"Well now, that's an easy matter to put right," said he, unconcerned at my offhand attitude, and within a moment he had whisked me across the crowded room to the honourable Alexander Forbes who made the necessary formalities.

"My dear Miss Alison," Alexander gave his elegant bow, "may I present my own younger son, the Honourable John Forres, Lieutenant in the Edinburgh Militia?"

The exquisite gave an elaborate if slightly mocking bow.

"And John, it is my greatest of pleasures to present Miss Alison Lamont, niece of Lady Elspeth Ballantyne, come all the way from Badenoch just for this ball, and some other family business, I believe"

John Forres gave another bow, so low that I feared, or rather hoped, that his trousers would split and embarrass him in front of the entire company, but the devil favours his own and instead he only delighted everybody with his elegance. He put out his hand but I declined the tease of a kiss and withdrew. Unfortunately, my most aloof formality was spoiled when Louise came close and stepped on my trailing gown so I jerked to a somewhat abrupt and very inelegant halt. I am sure that she did it deliberately, the minx.

"And this is Miss Louise Ballantyne," Alexander Forres seemed not a whit put out by Louise's forward behaviour.

The bow was just as low, but Louise did not pull back her hand, and Lieutenant Forres made the most of his opportunity. It must have been a good minute before he rose, but Louise did not mind in the least. There was no mistaking the sparkle in her eyes when she looked at me and no ambiguity in the look of triumph that I was too young to then understand. I learned though, as you will hear, by and by.

Lady Catriona had hired a small band to play for us, and once we started dancing, we did not stop save to nibble at the table of snacks or engage in light conversation. I cannot remember exactly what we danced, country reels, I believe, and the occasional Highland dance, complete with high screeches and the most intricate of footwork. The waltz did not make its way into Scotland for a year or so, as it was considered most indelicate. Honestly my dears, you have no idea how much hypocrisy ruled our lives when romantic affairs were considered normal, and only became a scandal if they were broadcast in public, yet to wear even a fraction of makeup was to chance being ostracised from all respectable society. Life is so different today.

Lady Catriona was not conservative in her taste, and soon we were executing a quadrille, with gentlemen and ladies all higgledy-piggledy together in that upstairs room. If I close my eyes I can picture it now, all the swirling kilts and flowing gowns, the sheen of exertion on noble foreheads, the bright eyes and laughing mouths and the shimmer of silk and satin. I can nearly hear the rhythmic drumming of feet on that polished floor and see the reflection of the chandelier on the windows. You might never have heard of the quadrille, a most enthralling dance with complex movements that you youngsters would never enjoy or probably understand, but while we were engaged, that Lieutenant John Forres arrived again, all tight breeches and pride, and seemed intent to partner me for the remainder of the evening.

A lady cannot object openly, as you know, but she can do her best to make a gentleman's life disagreeable if she so wishes, so I returned his pleasantries with formal disdain and rejected his advances with a politely cold shoulder.

"My dear Miss Alison," he said at length, stepping back, "I do hope that I have done nothing to offend you? Why in the Peninsula the society ladies were falling over themselves for only a whisper of our company..."

"Why, Mr. Forres! Were you in the Peninsula? How brave of you!" Louise had appeared like a perfumed ghost, and without a by-your-leave, she stepped between us as if she were taking a French prisoner from a battlefield.

Lieutenant Forres only looked surprised for a moment, and then he proffered his arm, which Louise accepted with a sidelong smile that I would have loved to have removed if I were not so much of a lady.

Now, I had no great liking for the dashing Lieutenant, but even then I knew when I was being insulted, and I resolved to strive with Cousin Louise for his attention. For the remainder of that evening, we competed for the favours of John Forres, and he lapped up our attention like a cat licks up the top of the cream. When he was not dancing with me, he was exchanging small talk with Louise, and when she was not whispering grave secrets behind her fan, she was watching us with her face green tinged with envy and those slanted eyes as malicious as a slighted politician.

"He's far better suited to me, you know," Louise told me as we circled around each other in one of those devilishly complicated quadrilles.

"I believe that he spoke to me first," I gave back, as sweetly as any serpent and we exchanged venomously insincere curtseys and parted, with John Forres smiling on us both indiscriminately. The smile I could thole, but when his hands followed his too-bold eyes I withdrew again, much to Louise's amusement.

"La, Lieutenant Forres," she said, "I do believe that you have scared the child. My cousin Alison is far too young for such adult pleasures."

"And you, madam, are not?"

"Indeed, sir that would entirely depend on the owner of the hand." Louise invited shamefully, but Lieutenant Forres acted more of the gentleman than I had expected when he merely smiled.

Louise did not appear pleased. "La, sir, but I believe that you are nothing but a tease."

"La, *madam*, but I am the best judge of my own actions." He withdrew for a space, and Louise's eyes wandered to the door which had opened to allow a small and compact group of men to enter.

I have few gifts in this world, but I am able to determine atmosphere, and as soon as these men walked into that room, I felt a shift. It was nothing tangible, nothing that I could put my finger on, but I knew that something had changed. So did Louise, of course, and she was pressing forward to see what was happening and what she could gain from the alteration.

"Who are these men?" I whispered to Alexander Forres, who had moved to my side like a guardian sheepdog to his prize lamb.

There were four of them, and although two wore uniforms, and two did not, there was no disguising the essential militariness of them all. Perhaps it was the compact way in which they stood or the quiet fire in their eyes, but they did not look out of place among the kilties and the scarlet jackets. I did not recognise their uniforms but that was not unexpected, given the amazing array of regiments and units that had been founded to fight Bonaparte's never ending war.

"They are French prisoners from the castle," Alexander Forres told me quietly, "out on parole. Some are allowed freedom from their confinement and Lady Catriona always invites a few to the Hogmanay ball."

"But they are the enemy," I did not hide my bewilderment.

Alexander's smile contained only fatherly tolerance. "My mother, Lady Catriona, insists that we have been friends with the French far longer than we have been enemies, and we shall be friends again just as soon as the warfare ceases." His laugh seemed to mock the entire edifice of society. "Anyway, Miss Alison, they are jovial company and they add a little spice to the evening, rather than just the usual manoeuvring for husbands, wives and fortunes."

I am still not sure if he was laughing at me, but Alexander was such a gentleman that it was even a pleasure to be teased by him. I accepted his comments with a smile and watched as the Frenchmen strolled in. Now you must understand that for most of my life, this country had been at war with France, and we had been brought up to regard Frenchmen as ogres that ate babies and spread republicanism, while Bonaparte was the devil's cockerel with a Corsican accent. However, we were also imbued with French culture, so that anybody with any pretence at education spoke French, while French furniture was never out of fashion, so you must excuse my mixed feelings when this quarter of Frenchmen entered our ball.

On first sight, I must admit to a certain disappointment. They were neither one thing nor the other, neither ogres nor icons of fashionable culture. I could not see a single forked tail or cloven hoof, although I confess that Louise was far more adept at investigating for such things, but neither did they bring the place alive with new ideas, indeed they looked decidedly ordinary. In different clothes, they could have fitted into the ranks of the kilties, or the militiamen.

It was more intriguing to watch the reaction of our soldiers. While the militia officers were a bit stand-offish, the Highlanders welcomed them like brothers in arms, extending a true hand of friendship and inviting them to make free with Lady Catriona's whisky, brandy and claret. The French responded in kind so that there was uproarious laughter from at least one section of the room.

Louise, of course, scented new men and hurried elegantly toward them, while Lady Catriona sat in her chair in the corner of the room, quietly smiling under her turban. She had created the scene and she obviously intended to enjoy it. Ordinary conventions did not concern her ladyship, so long as the basic proprieties were observed. Other ladies, as you will see by-and-by, were not quite so easy- natured.

Well, that evening passed in a haze of swirling tartan and emptying glasses, of sparkling conversation and hectic flirting, of rustling silk and drumming heels on the dance floor, until somebody announced that it was almost midnight. Of course, we all scurried to the decanters and then observed the sacred minute, standing with our brimming glasses in hand while Alexander counted off the seconds to the beginning of the New Year.

I can picture the scene as if it were yesterday, rather than sixty, or is it seventy-odd years ago? All the brave uniforms standing to attention with the eager young ladies at their side, Louise gripping the arm of John Forres as if he were a prize she had won at the local fair and the tallest and most personable of the Frenchmen edging ever closer with his lips slightly open and his eyes burning with Gallic ardour.

"Ten ... nine ... eight..." Alexander held an enormous gold watch in his hand as he solemnly intoned the seconds as if we could not see the massive grandfather clock only a few feet away.

"Seven ... six ... five..."

Louise gave a little scream of anticipation and sipped at her ratafia. That was a light wine, dears, favoured by ladies, and Louise could try so hard to appear ladylike when it suited her purpose. Society does not favour ratafia nowadays, which is a shame; it was an innocuous kind of drink and rarely did much harm.

"Four ... three ... two..."

There was a tremendous sense of anticipation in that room, with everybody holding their breath. Except for Louise, who was holding the arm of John Forres and giggling as the Frenchman whispered something in her ear.

"One!" Alexander raised his glass. "Happy New Year everybody, and let us hope that 1812 is successful and prosperous," I could see that he wanted to ask for a victorious conclusion to the war against Napoleon

Bonaparte, but for the sake of politeness to the French officers present, he refrained. "And let us all hope for a lasting and just peace."

"Success, prosperity and peace!" The gathering intoned solemnly, but when Louise lifted her lips for a New Year kiss, John Forres slipped free, grabbed hold of me and planted a flattering, but extremely unwelcome, kiss square on my mouth.

I must have screamed at this unwarranted assault, but it is difficult to make any real noise when somebody is effectively covering your lips. Louise, however, was not so restrained and she made some very unladylike remarks just as John released me. I looked at her in astonishment while the colour rushed to my face.

"Madam..." She had her hands on her hips and her head thrust forward so she looked just like one of the hens that scratched around the townships alongside the Calder River in Badenoch.

"Yes," I said. I was unhappy at the assault, but secretly quite pleased that a gentleman, of whatever character, had chosen me over my forward and quite beautiful cousin.

"Madam..." Louise repeated but stopped. After all, what could she say? Turning with a fine show of indignation, she quite accidentally twisted the heel of her shoe, slipped, and crashed against me.

We must have made a fine display as we fell in a flurry of skirts and tangled limbs, with our legs a-flailing legs and arms waving uselessly. Strangely it was the tall French officer who was first to offer assistance, raising Louise with a grace I still find it hard to fault, while John Forres merely smiled and thrust out an ineffectual hand while her Ladyship frowned beyond her fan.

"Whose fault was that?" Her Ladyship's voice had lost any pretence at amiability as the concordance quietened.

"I believe it was Miss Alison," Louise gave voice, rubbing at her ankle as the French officer directed her to a chair. She looked at me balefully.

"Then Miss Alison should leave the company," Lady Catriona pronounced. "Send for the sedan chair. The chairmen can carry her to Lady Elspeth's town house immediately. I will not tolerate such disgraceful scenes in the Forres Residence. This is Edinburgh, Miss Alison, and we have no place for your wild Highland ways."

Chapter Two

You may be used to the Highlands being lauded and Highlanders being treated with respect equal to people in any other part of this kingdom, but you must remember that this was 1811, before Queen Victoria chose to bless Caledonia with her presence. There were still memories of the rising of 1745, and in my time, Highlanders were reckoned as of no more account than Irishmen or Africans. They called us Donalds, among other less savoury things, and told tall tales of our backwardness and savagery, despite the many thousands of Highlandmen who were even then fighting their wars for them. For Lady Catriona to remark on my Highland blood was tantamount to a terrible insult, and one to which I could not reply, for it was only the truth. I had been born and raised among the mountains of Badenoch and was as Highland as peat.

There was no reprieve from such a pronouncement of rejection. In my youth, you see, we did not question the wisdom of our elders and betters. Indeed, we dared not, for the consequences could be ... well, I will leave that to your imaginations but.

It was unpleasant to be banished in disgrace, but to be honest I had experienced quite enough of Lady Catriona's ball. My anticipation had been disappointed, my hopes dashed and my lips assaulted. In truth, I was not unhappy to climb inside the padded and very ornate sedan chair and have the stalwart Highland chairmen lift me. I would have preferred to travel by coach, but I do not believe that Lady Catriona would have countenanced such luxury for somebody she obviously considered a blackguard and an out-and-out rogue. I also knew that I was in disgrace, and wondered what Lady Elspeth would say about the situation when I arrived back in her house. However much I reasoned that such things were probably not uncommon in such a cosmopolitan city as Edinburgh, and if I were home first, I would have the first opportunity to state my side of the argument, I knew that it was natural for Aunt Elspeth to take her daughter's side against me.

Such thoughts occupied me as the chairmen ported me up the wynd and into the bustle of the High Street. Tears were not far from my eyes as I considered Lady Elspeth's reaction, for I knew that Louise would put all the blame on my shoulders, and I would be doubly disgraced. I had no ideas what penalties her ladyship would inflict, but I suspected they might be grievous. She may even send me back to Badenoch, where my chances of finding a suitable husband were limited in the extreme.

However, events in the High Street soon chased the tears away and gave me much more serious matters to worry about than the displeasure of an eccentric old crone such as Lady Catriona and my stern but probably fair aunt.

I heard the roar before I saw anything untoward, for a sedan chair does not have the best of visibility and I was engaged in a monumental sulk, combined with great self- pity both for my present position and the niggling pain of what I was sure was a blister developing on the large toe of my left foot. So when the front chairman let his poles go with a thump, I only complained a little before I opened the door and peered out.

The High Street was in such a state of consternation that I thought the French had landed and was attempting to assault Edinburgh Castle. There were people everywhere, mostly youngsters in their teens and early twenties, shouting and gesticulating, using the most commonplace language I had ever heard, throwing rocks and bottles at the houses and at the poor Watchmen who attempted to restore peace, fighting with fists and feet and generally behaving as if there was no God and Lucifer had descended to claim the kingdom.

"Whatever is the commotion?" I enquired, but nobody seemed to take heed of me, even though I stamped my foot quite forcibly on the ground.

I could hear the chairmen talking, their Gaelic easily comprehensible to me, for Lady Catriona was correct in that at least. Being a native of the Highlands I understood the speech quite as well as I understood English.

"We can't get through that lot," one chairman said, pointing to the crowd.

"We'll have to, or Her Ladyship will have our jobs," the second reminded. "Lady Catriona is not the sort of person to give an order and not have it carried out" He added a few more comments about Lady Catriona which, although I agreed with, I think it best not to commit to paper at this time. They were certainly not fit for tender young ears, and I would have blushed if I was not perfectly pleased to hear the old harridan so insulted.

"Down the closes then," the first man said, and only then did he notice that I was standing outside the chair and listening to his conversation.

Switching to English, for he was naturally unaware that I spoke Gaelic, he gave the shortest and quite the most disrespectful bow I have ever seen. "We not going that way," he told me, jerking a stubby thumb at the mob, "we'll have to go through the closes and around the loch. It will take longer."

There was no by-your-leave, you'll notice, and no "my lady" or any other term of respect. Highlanders are like that; you have to earn their respect and if you give them an inch they'll take three yards, and anything else they can lay their hands on.

"You'll do as I tell you," I bristled, for I was young and full of fire and foolish spirit.

"Aye, right," the spokesman replied, with no thought at all for my dignity. "Just get in, sit tight and hold your tongue. God knows what these blackguards will do if they see Her Ladyship's sedan in the streets."

Nearly pushing me inside the chair, the Highlanders lifted it and ran to the nearest close – that's a narrow alleyway, dears, nearly unseating me in the process. I do not know the name of the dark ravine into which we plunged, but the smells were abominable and the darkness stygian. We could well have been in the Pit or any of the famous stews of London, but for all their caution, we had been seen.

Once again I heard the roar of the crowd, and something hard and heavy smashed from the side panel of the chair. I remember thinking that Her Ladyship would not be pleased with this disrespect even as I stifled a small scream.

"That's enough of that, you scoundrel!" The porter had returned to his native tongue, and he continued to berate the thrower in language that was quite choice and far too colourful for you ladies to know. We might not have been quite as ladylike in our youth as we pretended, for we did know the meanings of some of these horrid words. You, of course, should not.

Anyway, another missile clattered from the coachwork and the porter yelled again. "I know you, Hughie McIntosh, and I'll attend to you tonight when I'm not working."

The reply was confused as if the said Hugh McIntosh was drunk, but there was no mistaking the thunder of boots down the close and against the side of the sedan, rocking it dreadfully and quite upsetting my temper. Somebody yanked the door open and I peered out, to see a whole bunch of rogues staring in.

"Get you gone, you drunken blaggards!" the second coachman shouted, still holding the poles and trying to walk forward. "This lady is under our protection and she's done you no harm at all!"

Until that second I had been annoyed and intrigued, but now I began to feel fear. There must have been twenty people in that mob and all appeared to come from the very dregs of society. Malice oozed from every predatory face, and I cannot repeat one word of what they said. Some spoke in Gaelic, some in Edinburgh Scots, but they seemed to be united in the common purpose of causing as much mischief as possible.

"Tip her out!"

A dozen grimy hands descended on the sedan, until my coachmen, Highland heroes both, placed it ungently on the ground and pushed them back with great shouts and violent action.

"Run, Miss Alison," the front chairman said. "We can't hold them for long and there's no knowing what they might do. Run!"

I hesitated of course, between the devil of that crowd and the deep blue sea of the dark closes of old Edinburgh, and, I am loath to admit, somewhere within me there was the genuine desire to stay and help my impolite porters.

"Run, woman!" the second chairman ordered and gave me a push in the back to help me on my way.

For the second time that evening I stumbled, but I fear helped me recover and I lifted my skirts and ran down that close as fast as my legs and my oh-so-fashionable high heeled shoes would allow.

Now, you girls nowadays live in a very civilised world, with gas lighting in the streets and piped water in nearly every house. In my time Old Edinburgh did not have such conveniences, so the close that I ran down was dark, foul and dangerous. I had only a vague knowledge of where I was going, but I knew that I had to leave the Old Town, cross the Earthen Mound and reach the graceful squares of the New Town where my Aunt Elspeth would be waiting to greet me with cakes and tea, or more likely a verbal assault that would blister my ears. Either was preferable to the deep darkness of that terrible lane or the horror of the mob at my heels.

You will notice that I had no thought of returning to the Forres Residence. Lady Catriona had sent me away, so away I must go, and quickly, my dears. Disobedience was not so much frowned upon as quickly and effectively squashed.

That close descended steeply, to open on to a winding street whose name I quite forget, but which was crammed with more raucous youths celebrating the advent of a new year by riot and dissipation.

Conspicuous in my bright dress and fashionable cloak, I tried to hide, but somebody caught sight of me and I was soon running again, with my heels sliding on the cobbled ground and my ankles screaming their protest at this ill treatment.

The noise behind me diminished in direct proportion to the darkness of my surroundings and I realised that my feet were sinking into something deeper than the normal noxious surface of Edinburgh's ground. I hesitated, unsure whether to continue, but a glance over my shoulder revealed an orange light over the city, and I feared that the whole of Edinburgh was aflame with the mob in charge like some hydra-headed republican monster.

I might have sobbed then, but I cannot recall exactly, but I do know that I looked outward for the lights and security of the New Town. They were there, plain and serene as a summer's morning, but despite all my efforts, I seemed to be no closer. I plunged on, holding up the trailing skirt of my gown that descended beneath my cloak, and felt something sucking at my shoes.

"Mud," I said gloomily, and plunged on, hoping that I could reach the Earthen Mound and cross the physical and metaphysical chasm that divided Edinburgh's two worlds.

Unfortunately, my dears, my sense of direction has never been good. I thrust myself into that mud with my feet sinking deeper and my heart pumping in a most unladylike manner, but although I did not realise it, I was moving ever further from my goal. The Earthen Mound and my road to Aunt Elspeth's lay to the east, but I was heading west.

I only became aware of my predicament when I saw the great sheet of water stretching before me, rippling in the starlight. If I were a man I would have sworn, but of course, I did not. Instead, I nearly gave way to a fit of temper, which did no good at all but only served to exhaust me further.

"I will follow the banks of this loch," I told myself, "and it will take me to Princes Street, for we drove that way only this afternoon."

Accordingly, I kept on until the mud sucked off my right shoe and I fell, for the third time that night. By now I had no idea for how long

I had been moving, but my legs were aching and mud covered me from my face downward. I was sobbing, wishing that John Forrest had chosen to kiss anybody but me, and wondering if I were destined to spend the entire night outside this God forsaken city.

It was cold. I had forgotten just how bitter a winter's night could be, and I shivered.

"Oh just let me go home," I prayed.

The noise from the city had long since faded everywhere but in my memory, so I felt as if I were the last women left in the world as I struggled along in the dark, with that rippling water a barrier between me and sanctuary and the thought of the predatory mob in the rear.

The cry of a goose was terribly lonely and I sank down, holding my head in my hands and nearly giving way to despair. I didn't of course, for I knew that I was only a few miles from safety, but when you are young and alone and in a strange place, the imagination can take control of your senses and you create all sort of terrible things that reality dispels.

It was then that I saw a faint yellow glow reflecting from the dark waters.

"What's that¿Who's there?"' I said the words faintly, not really sure that I had seen anything and not really sure if I wanted a reply, for anybody out here at this time of night must be a desperate character. Brought up on the fearful gothic novels that were prevalent at the time, I could imagine any sort of horror, ghosts or vampires or even some of the phantom dogs or water kelpies of my Highland childhood.

I nearly collapsed when there came a bold reply.

"Hello!"

I halted, unsure whether to go on or to return. There I was, barely eighteen years old and lost beside a dirty loch half way between old and new Edinburgh and with a strange and definitely male voice was calling to me. I was in that wonderful state where reality and imagination merge, when I was unsure if I was dreaming or awake, real or unreal, the twilight of existence where even the solid seems insubstantial.

The voice sounded again. "Hello?"

I sat tight, saying nothing and hoping for solitude nearly as much as I hoped for discovery.

A lantern flickered, the reflection of its light on the placid waters disturbing a goose into explosive flight.

Still, I waited, unsure what to do. There is no disease worse than uncertainty, my dears. My advice to you is to decide on a course of action and carry it through. It is always far better to regret what you have done that regret that you lacked the courage to do anything.

For a third time, that male voice sounded. "Hello? Is there anybody there?" The lamplight circled, flicking over the water and through the sedges on the bank, casting weird shadows and making the surrounding dark even blacker by contrast.

Still, I did nothing, with my opportunity for help fast passing me by. Was I scared? Yes, but not of that unknown voice, more of my own fears. I thought of pirates and smugglers and sorners, but never of the truth.

The light vanished, somebody muttered something that I could not catch and then I was alone again in the somehow greater darkness and I felt lonelier than I had ever felt before.

"Help!" The word was out before I knew it. "Please help me!"

But there was no friendly beam of light. The darkness remained as dark, the solitariness as solitary and my feelings as confused as before, except that now I knew that I was scared and after that hint of companionship I desperately sought human company. I could smell smoke, so in my disordered mind, there must be a house nearby. I did not consider that we were no distance of Edinburgh, which had well earned its sobriquet of Auld Reekie.

"Hello! Please help me!"

I blundered forward, hoping for the source of that light. I had passed the point of caring about my appearance or my dignity, all I wanted was somewhere to shelter, a fire to sit beside and the sound of a human voice. Ignoring the mud that splashed higher with every lumbering step, ignoring the sodden mess of my best cloak and the only ball gown that I had ever possessed, I staggered on, until I fell against the harsh wall of a hut.

My mind only fixed on one thing. A hut meant shelter from the night. True it was humble, but I was no great lady to disdain simplicity, but a Highland girl lost near Edinburgh. Fumbling around the walls, I found a door handle.

Yanking it open, I nearly fell inside, aware only of a welcoming fire and the scent of something that could have been newly baked bread.

The tall man stared at me in astonishment.

"What the devil!"

And I looked into the angry eyes of Willie Kemp.

There was no mirror inside that hut but I can imagine what sort of picture I must have presented. Hatless, for I had lost my hat in the mad dash from the sedan, and shoeless, for I had lost both while blundering along the loch side; with mud thick on my cloak and my person, and dripping with water, I must have appeared more a ragged beggar woman than the young lady of fashion who left home a few short hours before.

"Who the devil are you?" Willie Kemp asked.

As I stared back at him with my mouth working and my clothes leaving a spreading puddle on his floor, I remembered what Louise had said about this man. He was a strange creature, a solitary man who spent his time making machines that did not work, and now I had barged into his hut beside the loch.

"I am Alison Lamont," I told him, and for reason, I added, "from Badenoch."

"Was it you yelling a few minutes ago?" He remained a few steps from me, standing beside a very handsome fire. I could see the breadth of his shoulders and the line of light on a jaw that was more stubborn than I liked. Not that I really cared, of course, but one does tend to notice such things, even with men as coarse and uncouth and tall as Willie Kemp.

"I asked you a question." There was no doubting the authority in his tone, which I resented as he was a mere tinker and I was the niece of Lady Elspeth Ballantyne

I resolved to be as stiffly standoffish as I knew how. "I am lost," I wailed. "I can't find my way home."

I did not see him move, but he was there to help me on to the only chair in that shed, and he was easing the cloak from my shoulders and tutting at my lack of shoes and the shocking condition of my feet on such a biting winter's night.

I was shivering as the reaction of my adventures hit home, and I hardly objected when he placed a great mug of soup in my hand.

You're cold" he said, and although his voice was deep, it was also surprisingly cultured.

I nodded. I knew that I should leave at once rather than be alone in the presence of an unknown man, but I was too frightened and too cold and too exhausted to think straight. I was, you will please remember, only eighteen years old and unsure of my surroundings.

Willie Kemp seemed unsure what to do. He watched me for a moment, frowning, and then he shook his head. "Well, you'd better get out of these wet things," he said, "or else you'll catch your death of cold."

I looked up, suddenly frightened as all the gothic stories returned. I could feel the hammer of my heart and realised that I was indeed alone with a strange man in an out of the way place and nobody knew where I was. "No," I whispered, and his frown deepened.

"You are cold," he said, and his voice was as harsh as a metal bar running across a granite cliff. "You are tired and you are wet. Unless you change into something dry and warm, you will catch a cold, if not pneumonia." He disappeared for a few moments, returning with what looked like a bundle of old cloth.

"I'll go away," he said, "and you put these on. I'll knock before I return."

Ungrateful wretch that I was, I said "no" unthinkingly, but the prospect of dry clothing was too great a temptation, even for such a headstrong miss as I was. As soon as Willie Kemp was outside, I placed the chair behind the door to ensure that it was secure and peeled off my clothing.

I was very lucky that the fashion in Edinburgh that year was for simple gowns, but even so, have you ever disrobed from a sodden ball gown without even a fumbling servant girl to help? I struggled with buttons and hooks, fought my frustration over eyes and stays, and eventually, and without a thought for Willie Kemp, stood stark in front of the fire. Strangely I lingered for a while, allowing the flames to ease away some of my chill before I turned to the clothing that Willie Kemp had given me.

I could have cried. Rather than the fashionable apparel that I was used to wearing, he had given me nothing but rough homespun, with not even a hint of an undergarment to protect my tender skin. If I say 'chafing' you will know what I mean, girls, without me needing to elaborate.

Hesitantly, and hoping that everything was clean, I hauled on a pair of trousers that were far too large for me and fumbled clumsily with the fly buttons. The very idea of doing such a thing was revolting, but necessity demanded that I wear such creations, so I had no choice. There was a long linen shirt, thank the Lord, which was softer than I perhaps deserved for my ingratitude, and then a thick jacket of some harsh material. I was only glad that Louise was not there to see me, and then I wondered what Aunt Elspeth would say.

I realised that Mr. Kemp had been knocking on the door for some minutes, but I resolved to let him wait a trifle longer while I rolled up the trouser legs to a more manageable length and folded back the cuffs of the jacket. Only then did I haul back the chair, and Mr. Kemp came in. He was dripping with wet, for it was raining again, and he stopped at the sight of me.

"Do you feel better?"

"These are very rough," I said. "Do you have nothing more suitable for a lady?"

"These are all I have," Mr. Kemp said quietly. Without any fuss, he lifted my discarded gown and spread it on some contraption of metal poles he had erected beside the fire. I gasped and tried to hide my underthings, but he lifted them with the same unconcern and placed them to dry as if it was the most natural thing in the world.

"Were you going far?" Mr. Kemp asked, and although I had resolved to tell him nothing, I unfolded the whole story, from my tiff with Louise to Lady Catriona's expulsion, the riot in Edinburgh and my miserable experience by the loch. He listened without comment, giving an occasional encouraging nod when I faltered, and only when I had completed the tale did he speak

"You have had a sorry night," he said, solemnly, "but you are warm now, and safe enough here."

"But sir," I said, "my reputation..."

His smile was gentle. "You need not fear for your reputation with me, Miss Lamont. I am known as an eccentric, not as a lady's man."

I had never met a man who was so direct and so accepting of his own position in the world. "You may realise that, Mr. Kemp, but others..."

"Others will talk whatever you say and whatever you do, Miss Lamont, and we both know that to be true. However, we may minimise any damage by keeping our behaviour beyond reproach."

"I fully intend to do that, Mr. Kemp," I replied, frostily, for I did not like the way that this mechanic, or whatever he was, seemed to be taking control of the situation.

"It is late, Miss Lamont," Mr. Kemp did not respond to my mood. I thought that perhaps he did not understand it, or he may have been afraid of me, as I came from such an elevated position in society compared to his. "And you are tired. You may sleep here tonight and complete your journey tomorrow."

I shook my head. "I can hardly do that, Mr. Kemp," I said, "for then my reputation will indeed be ruined." All the same, it was comfortable in front of this huge fire, with Mr. Kemp's thick clothing covering me on the outside and his soup warming me inside. I vowed to remain just a few moments more, or until my own clothes were dry, and then I would go back outside and, hopefully, Mr. Kemp would direct me on the correct route to the New Town.

Nevertheless, I did not protest when Mr. Kemp spread a blanket over me, or when he placed his own jacket, carefully folded, under my head.

It may have been the sound of calling geese that wakened me or the perfume of something fragrant slowly cooking, but I stretched with a sense of well- being, opened my eyes and immediately wondered where I was. I did not recognise my surroundings, not the rough stone walls, or the shaped shelves above my head, or the piled up pieces of metal that lay between my bed and the smouldering fire where the pot gave that delicious fragrance. Only when the large man smiled down at me did I remember where I was, and where I had spent the night.

"Oh my Lord," I said, sitting up in bed and looking down at myself. I had no need to worry for I was still fully clothed, and had a couple of blankets piled on me to boot. "I've been here all night!"

"You have," said Mr. Kemp, "sleeping sound and snoring softly."

"I do not snore," I denied, but it was the far more important matter of my reputation that concerned me.

"Breakfast in ready," Mr. Kemp told me. "There is warm water for you to wash, and your own clothes are clean and dry."

I looked up and saw that Mr. Kemp had been busy while I slept. He must have washed the mud from my cloak and my gown, and both lay clean and dry on that metal contraption beside the still living fire. He had also gone to the trouble of retrieving my shoes from the mud, although how he had done so in the dark I could not imagine. They too lay clean and dry, standing at the foot of my bed.

"Mr. Kemp," I said, and stopped. What could I say to an eccentric mechanic who had treated me with such kindness, yet spoken so bluntly?

"Miss Lamont," he raised his eyebrows in reply.

"If you will kindly grant me some privacy I shall certainly rise now and get myself ready." I looked around the room, hoping to see a necessary convenience, but there was none.

Mr. Kemp spared me the embarrassment of having to ask. 'There is a door some short distance behind you,' he said quietly. "If you would kindly step through, you will find a pitcher and ewer, warm water, soap and the other necessities of your morning needs." He bowed slowly, a tall, tanned man with patched homespun clothing and hands the size of shovels. "I will leave you in peace for an hour or so. Your breakfast is keeping warm by the fire."

He left very quietly for such a big man, and once again I pulled the chair to the door in case he should return unannounced, although by now I was beginning to have some trust for Mr. Kemp. Did I like him? I do not know the answer to that question, for at eighteen I concealed my feelings from everybody, myself most of all.

The small room was exactly as he described, but he had not mentioned the mirror which seemed too large for use in shaving, so I suspected that he had brought it in especially for me. I did not see Willie Kemp as one of these preening dandies who spent so much time admiring themselves in front of the mirror to ensure they were perfect in feature and form. I recollected his long, saturnine face and shook my head. No, he was certainly no dandy, not with that unfashionably neat queue and the unruly whiskers that barely extended past his ears.

There were two candles already alight in that windowless room, so I watched myself as I washed in that deliciously warm water, with a soap that produced a lather equal to anything I had experienced at home. It smelled of primroses, which was also quite unusual for a man, so I wondered anew at this eccentric.

It was easier to remove Mr. Kemp's clothing than it had been to don it, but as the last of the heavy cloth fell to the ground I smiled. It had been a strange experience altogether, to wear something that habitually covered the body of a man. The thought was strangely disturbing, so I discarded it, although I suspected that the images might return later.

The rough material had rubbed parts of my body that were normally protected, so I examined myself for permanent damage but found none. Only a few red patches here and there, particularly on my hips. I turned sideways. I quite liked my curves, although I seldom had an opportunity to observe them in privacy. There had been four of us sharing one room in Badenoch, and Aunt Elspeth had insisted that I share with Louise in Edinburgh, while there were always maids running at the back of me with unwanted advice and fiddling fingers.

I turned in front of Willie Kemp's mirror, seeing my quite well-shaped breasts and the smooth curve of my flank, the swell of hips and my slightly too large bottom. Was there ever a woman born who was happy with her shape? Are you, my dears? Take off your clothes now, this very minute, and look in the mirror. Write down what you think, and then ask somebody close, a sister perhaps, or your most trusted maid, to tell you what she really thinks. And then fight your natural urge to slap her soundly and believe her words rather than your own.

I longed for somebody to ask such advice, but there was nobody. My mother, may God rest her soul, would never have countenanced my looking in a mirror or any other sort of self- observation. I shudder to think of the consequences, but what harm is there in such an innocent pastime? God made us all, so we should surely be allowed to enjoy one of His finest creations.

There was a perverse thrill about standing naked knowing that there was a strange man standing so close, but also an element of apprehension, so after my initial few minutes of luxurious tension, I hurried as best I could. My own clothes were dry, and after being beside the fire all night, deliciously warm, which made a nice change for mother always insisted on us freezing. It built character, she claimed, although I always suspected that it was more likely to lead to pneumonia.

Fully dressed, I attempted to do something with the tangled explosion of my hair. Mr. Kemp either had strange tastes or a profusion of lady friends, for there was a full dressing set by the mirror, and I hauled and combed and brushed madly until I had imposed a semblance of order on my ugly black head. God knows how I envied Louise her beautiful blonde hair, while mine was as black as the Earl of Hell's waistcoat and as liable to snarl as a bramble bush in an autumn gale.

I was extraordinarily disappointed that the outer room in that shed, and there were only the two rooms, was empty of Mr. Kemp. However, my breakfast was laid out on a plate by the fire, and I ate the fresh fish, presumably newly caught from the loch, and the eggs, with as much relish as I would any delicacy from Lady Elspeth's table. And Mr. Kemp had provided a knife and fork as well, which astonished me as I expected such a class of people to eat with their fingers.

The cutlery was of good quality silver too but had obviously been stolen as there was an embossed coat of arms on the handle of each. Not recognising the symbol of the crown and crossed swords, I wondered, briefly, who the rightful owner might be. I smiled, wondering if Mr. Kemp had been the thief, but somehow I could not imagine him sneaking through the window of some great house to filch a handful of forks. More likely he had bought it cheap in some corner pawnshop in the Auld Town.

As if my some magic spell, Mr. Kemp knocked on the door the moment I had finished my breakfast.

"Come in," I sang, for I knew it was he.

Taking one step inside, Mr. Kemp stopped and looked directly at me. "You clean up remarkably well," he said.

"And what do you mean by that?" I prepared to defend myself against an insult. One does, after living with five brothers and sisters, and then sharing a room with Louisa.

"Last night you came in as a gaberlunzie, a ragged orphan of the storm. This morning you are pretty as any picture, a young lady fit to grace a palace, and far too good for my humble home."

"I think you are making game of me, Mister Kemp." I was unsure if he was mocking me, but I suspected that he was, although I could not think of a method or retaliating except to turn my shoulder. Which I did, of course, but he seemed not to notice.

"Indeed I am not," Mr. Kemp said, smiling at me.

I resolved to be polite but distant, as suited a lady speaking with an obliging servant. "You have been very helpful," I favoured him with a small smile, "and I am sure that my aunt, Lady Elspeth Ballantyne, will thank you with some suitable remuneration when she sees fit. But now, pray, show me the way back to the New Town of Edinburgh."

"Pray step outside, Miss Lamont," Mr. Kemp invited and opened the door wide.

Now you must remember that I had stumbled on this shack in the dark of a December night, and I had no idea of my location. But once I stepped outside I knew exactly where I was, and how foolish I had been.

That first day of January 1812 was undoubtedly one of the most beautiful in creation. The Lord had seen fit to bless us with a bright curve of clear skies and a high sky that enhanced everything beneath it. I stood outside that shed and wondered at the delights of the day.

In the light of morning, the North Loch seemed far less formidable an obstacle, more like a tiny Highland Lochan or a muddy duck pond in a lowland village than a real loch. Indeed I wondered how such an insignificant stretch of water could have caused me so many problems only a few hours earlier. Overlooking the loch, Edinburgh Castle dominated everything beneath its grey battlements and tall stone buildings. The multi-crossed flag of Union floated high and even from here I could see the splashes of scarlet as the garrison took their stations behind the parapet.

Straggling downward from the castle were the irregular rooftops of the Old Town, with the Forres Residence dominating the top section. I sighed and turned around. I was perhaps thirty yards from Princes Street, the outlier of the New Town. I could nearly have thrown a stone across the loch, and then I would have been home in ten or fifteen minutes.

"So close!"

"Yet so far," Mr. Kemp seemed to have read my thoughts. "You see, Miss Lamont, to reach your destination you would have to skirt the loch, which would have taken quite some time." He pointed out the ragged edge of the loch, with its waving reeds and the vast patches of boggy mud that I had experienced the previous night.

"So, Mr. Kemp, what must I do?"

"You must wait here for the sedan-chair men."

The reply confused me. "Which sedan- chair men, Mr. Kemp? There is nobody who knows I am here save you."

His smile was infuriatingly enigmatic, but his reply was as open as everything else about him. "When you were sleeping, Miss Lamont, I took the liberty of walking to Lady Elspeth's house to explain your situation. I knew that Her Ladyship would be worrying about you. She promised to send her chair for you this morning, once her servants have recovered from their excesses of last night."

I stared at him. "So Aunt Elspeth knows?"

"She does," he confirmed. "Otherwise she would be immensely concerned."

Sinking down into the chair, I dropped my head into my hands. For once my melodrama was genuine and not copied from a Gothic romance. Aunt Elspeth would be most upset that I had spent the night in such a place and with such a person. I did not know how she would react, but certainly she would be less than pleased at my conduct.

I looked up at Mr. Kemp. "You have ruined me," I said. "You have ruined both my reputation and my future happiness."

He smiled. "I do not believe the situation is quite as bad as you imagine," he said. "Lady Elspeth may appear stern, but she is no ogre. She will understand the situation, and in the meantime, you must remain here with me."

I shook my head, content in my own despair. "How can you know about Lady Elspeth?" My, but I could be quite the high-born lady when I tried, could I not? Looking back, I am not sure whether to be amused or embarrassed at my own performance, and I still want to hide my face in shame at my treatment of that poor man. Poor Willie Kemp, God bless him, but how I did rail that morning!

"You are only a vagabond of the loch, a mechanic who lives in a tumbledown shack," I said, pointing out the shed in which he had cared for me the previous night. "How could you possibly understand the culture of your betters?"

He stood with his head titled slightly to one side, listening solemnly to my curtain lecture.

"You had no right to approach Lady Elspeth," I told him, and I am sure that I wagged my finger, "imagine! A man in your position knocking at the door of a titled Lady! What must she have thought! And what airs and graces you must have apportioned to yourself!"

At that time, you see, I thought only of myself and of the shame that I must now endure. I gave not a whit's consideration of the trouble that Mr. Kemp had been to, of the care he had taken of me, of his long and lonely walk through the dark of a winter's night, or even of my occupying his only bed while he spent the night outdoors, which he most certainly had.

"Have you finished?" He asked, smiling at me in that most disconcerting manner.

I nodded, for I had run out of breath and out of words.

"In that case, you had better prepare yourself, Miss Lamont, for I see Lady Elspeth's chairmen approaching now."

I had imagined that Mr. Kemp would have greeted the sedan chair porters like brothers, and they would have partaken of early morning ale together or perhaps whisky as we do in the north, but instead, he stepped back and allowed me to take over the proceedings.

I greeted the porters with courtesy, of course, for one must always be polite with servants, even when dismissing them, and I slid into the padded seat with all the dignity that I could muster, given the circumstances. With barely a nod to Mr. Kemp, I gave the order and the chairmen lifted me and began the long porterage to the New Town. As I peered from my curtained window, I saw Mr. Kemp watching, still with that curious smile on his face. Why, I asked myself, if one must always be polite to servants, had I allowed myself to scold him in such a manner? It was almost as if I treated him as a brother, or worse.

When he lifted his arm in farewell I could not meet his eyes, but looked away, to see the hut in which I had spent the night and the strange mechanical contraption that sat at its side. No doubt that was the machine on which the eccentric Mr. Kemp wasted so much of his time.

But I did not care, of course, for I had more immediate concerns, such as my impending interview with Aunt Elspeth, and how badly that infernal mud had treated my gown and shoes.

Chapter Three

I had expected an uncomfortable half hour with Aunt Elspeth, but I had not expected anything like the interview that she gave me. Perhaps we did have more freedom, perhaps even wild ways in the north, but at least there I was treated with some sort of respect. We all had a place in society and acted accordingly, but by the time Aunt Elspeth was finished with me I knew that there was no place except that which she assigned to me, and that was probably somewhere I did not want to be.

Taking me into the withdrawing room, she dismissed all the servants, but allowed Louisa to stay, which I considered grossly unfair. Her expression was one of the utmost distaste as she looked me up and down, from the top of my hatless head to the toes of my scuffed boots. "Your behaviour," she began, with her voice as frosty as any winter night, "was worse than abominable. By making a spectacle of yourself you insulted Lady Catriona, you made a fool out of me and you threw my hospitality back in my face."

I said nothing. At that moment I felt only like weeping, but somehow I realised that that particular weapon of defence would not work on this occasion. Lady Elspeth Ballantyne was perhaps forty, with the straight back and dignified bearing that only an Edinburgh matriarch could show. Mistress of her household, she always dressed in a simple yet refined manner, with the most cultured of clothes that somehow seemed practical as she took sole charge of her house and all that was in it. Unfortunately, that included me.

We stood there, with the three great windows open to the greenery of Queen Street Gardens and beyond toward the Firth of Forth, and the elegant furniture revealing everything of Aunt Elspeth's life. I tried to concentrate on the Sevres porcelain and fine furniture, but it was impossible to avoid the steel in Aunt Elspeth's eyes, particularly when she gripped my arms and pulled me toward her.

"You shamed me by your behaviour," Aunt Elspeth said, and I tried to look away but failed. Honestly, you would think that I had voiced republican tendencies the way that she carried on.

"My goodness, girlie, if you were a few years younger I would take a birch rod to you, and even now I am tempted..." The thought was so appalling that I shuddered. Louisa sat upright on the sofa in obvious delight and I saw her face brighten hopefully as she looked toward my aunt. For an instant I imagined myself... but that is an image that I will spare you, my dears. Suffice to say that the threat itself was enough to reduce me to tears, which was probably the ogre's intention. "We will let that drop for now," Aunt Elspeth said, and I sensed Louisa's disappointment.

I hoped for a reprieve then, but Aunt Elspeth was only drawing breath for the next assault. "You left the Forres residence attended by two servants and managed to lose them. You remained away all night, which could have kept me half demented with worry. You returned looking like a gaberlunzie girl after spending the night unchaperoned with a man..." Aunt Elspeth stopped, obviously at a loss what to say. "By heavens girlie, if the full details of your misbehaviour ever get out, I do not know what sort of damage it will do to your reputation. We are lucky that the town is talking about the riot that occurred last night and not of the indiscretions of some foolish Highland child."

She shook her head. "You must write a full letter of apology to Lady Catriona, and I will read it before it is dispatched."

I nodded and began to move away but Aunt Elspeth dragged me back, to the delight of my loving cousin. "Oh, I have not finished yet, Miss Alison. My servants tell me that when they arrived you were addressing Willie Kemp most terribly."

Why Willie Kemp, I thought, idly. Why not Kemp, or Mr. Kemp? What was different about that maddeningly serene mechanic?

"They told me that they could hear you, shouting like a Newhaven fishwife, from the other side of the loch."

I tried to hang my head as my face burned with genuine shame. Had I really been that bad? Fishwives were notorious for their vitriolic language, so perhaps I should have been proud of my verbal display, but with Aunt Elspeth's wide eyes glaring into mine, I was anything but. "Yes, Aunt Elspeth," I said, as meekly as if I had indeed been soundly birched. I could still sense Louise enjoying my humiliation, and I resolved to involve her in some way. "But it was not all my fault, Aunt Elspeth. Louise was quite as guilty as I. It was Louise that knocked me down, and not me her, and she was so intent on cutting out John Forres that she was positively green eyed whenever he looked at me. And she was particularly jealous when he kissed me at the sound of the bells..."

I had to stop, aware that I had probably said far too much and had incriminated myself in admitting that stolen kiss. Louise was looking at me with something like horror, and for a second I felt sweet revenge, but that soon disappeared as I was nearly sorry for her.

My outburst had stopped Aunt Elspeth in mid- sentence.

I do not think I have ever experienced a silence quite as intense as I did in that instant. I could hear every whirr of the grandmother clock that stood in the angle of the wall and could even make out the grinding of wheels as a coach passed the window. The sound of the horse's hooves seemed to beat time as Aunt Elspeth's grip tightened on my upper arms. For a second I thought that she was going to slap me and I quailed.

"Indeed," Aunt Elspeth said and repeated herself. "Indeed."

I waited for the world to end, but instead, Aunt Elspeth began to laugh. It was a lightning change of mood that quite threw me off guard so that for a second I believed that all was right with the world and I was forgiven my trespasses of the previous evening. However, my dears, in this world everything has to be paid for, especially moments of happiness, and one must learn to keep control of one's tongue. It is a hard lesson for a girl like I was, and, I suspect, for most females in our family.

"So you think fit to bandy words with me, young miss." Aunt Elspeth laughed again, and I permitted myself a small smile, although I was aware that Louise was nearly frozen to the couch with her face a picture of horror that could well have acted as a frontispiece to any gothic book.

"Well now, so John Forres bestowed a kiss upon you, and not upon Louise," Aunt Elspeth continued. "So be it indeed." Dropping her grip from my arms, she walked the full length of the room, with her skirt swishing against her legs and that clock still ticking away the terrible seconds. When she returned she seemed to have made a momentous decision, although to me it sounded just like an excuse to get me away for a while.

"Miss Alison, I wish you to wash and change, for you certainly will not be wearing that ball gown for quite some time. Put on something more practical for the weather, for I want you to return to Willie Kemp's cottage."

I stared at her. "Return to Willie Kemp? Whatever for? The man is nothing more than a mechanic, and eccentric to boot."

Aunt Elspeth nodded. "That may be one opinion of the good Mr. Kemp, but he certainly helped you last night. He gave you hospitality, he gave you shelter and he gave you food. He advised me of your whereabouts, which relieved me of a great deal of anxiety, and what did you give him in return?"

I shook my head. "I gave him nothing, Aunt Elspeth."

"Indeed you did. You gave him ingratitude and unladylike abuse. So now you will return, you will thank him for his assistance and you will offer your most sincere apologies for your behaviour."

I shook my head, proud as a Highland Lucifer that I was, and quite unable to see what was happening in this household. My, but I was naïve in my youth, although I believed that I knew everything there was to know. It is a strange fact, my dears, that youthful ignorance convinces us that we know everything, but the more experience we have, the more we realise that we do not know much at all.

"I cannot do that," I said, putting on my most stubborn of faces, the same face that always worked at home. "I cannot apologise to a mere mechanic!"

Aunt Elspeth leant closer with a curious frown on her face. "Perhaps not to a mechanic, Miss Alison," she told me, "but you can and you will apologise to Willie Kemp. You will carry your letter to him first thing tomorrow morning." That cold steel was back in her voice, so I knew that I would indeed apologise to Mr. Willie Kemp, and be glad to do so.

"And now, young lady," I was pleased to see that Aunt Elspeth was addressing Louise in a tone of voice quite as severe as she had used on me. Louise nodded, unable to meet these terrible eyes. "We have things to discuss, have we not?"

I waited hopefully, fully expecting to see a scene, but Aunt Elspeth turned to me. "Did I not give you something to do?" she asked, so quietly that I knew it was best to leave.

"Yes, Aunt Elspeth," I said, and before I knew it I was outside that door and nearly running up the stairs to the bedroom that I shared with Louise.

I still do not fully know what was said or done in the withdrawing room after I left, but I do know that Louise was in fits of tears when she returned, and she threw herself upon the bed in a perfect fury of sorrow. I left her to her howling and snuffling, for I had to compose a letter that contained an apology suitable for the eyes of Aunt Elspeth yet one that a man of probably limited education would understand.

"I hate you," Louise said, from behind the muffling veil of tears and the pillow that she pressed against her face to still the sobs. "Oh I hate you, Alison Lamont, and I hope that you are never happy in your life."

"Why, thank you; I hate you too." I gave a small curtsey, for after living with a brood of brothers and sisters I did not take the wild passion of the moment as seriously as Louise intended. Perhaps I should have been more considerate of her feelings, but with an early morning meeting with a low- born mechanic pressing on my mind, I could not afford to dwell on her black temper.

We spent the remainder of that day in silence, save for Louise's sobs and snufflings, so I once I had written my letter, I buried my nose in a book except for when we ate, and the meals were as sombre affairs as any funeral. More sombre, in fact, for in the Highlands such affairs are enlivened with plenty whisky, which loosens tongues and creates songs. There was no singing at Aunt Elspeth's table that day, and neither whisky, wine or kindness for the disgraced young ladies of the household. "You two had better repair to bed," Aunt Elspeth told us gravely, "and remember, Alison, you have a task first thing tomorrow."

Aunt Elspeth had supplied us with a dressing table and all the paraphernalia that our generation thought essential to a woman's looks. As soon as we had breakfasted next morning, I left Louise to her perennial sobbing, disrobed to my underthings and slid onto the stool. The adventures of the day before had not damaged me as much as I had feared, for save for a slight shadowing of my eyes that was created by tiredness, the same face reflected today that I had seen yesterday and the day before.

All the same, I resolved that Mr. Willie Kemp should not see me in such a bad light for the second time in succession. Two days past he had seen a waif from the storm, a refugee of the riots, but today he should see a lady, despite the fact that my clothes would of necessity be humble and hard wearing. He should also see my face at its best, not spattered with mud, rain and tears.

Accordingly, I selected the chief of the potions and perfumes and ointments that were arrayed across that table. There was a small glass marked *Royal Tincture of Peach Kernels* and there was a bottle of bloom of roses, which I knew to be rouge, which was not quite as fashionable as it once was. There was Olympian Dew eye lotion, which I knew made even the most tired of eyes sparkle, and pimpernel water for the complexion.

As I worked on myself, admiring my face in the mirror and ignoring the constant snuffling and whining from my beloved cousin, I wondered how best I should apologise to Mr. Kemp. Should I appear humble and contrite, or honest and misunderstood? Either way, the entire process should not take long, for what did a young lady like me have in common with a grubby-fingered mechanic? Nothing really, so I should be there and back within a couple of hours.

I had hoped that Aunt Elspeth would lend me her carriage for the short hop across to Mr. Kemp's hut, but she had borrowed that for some mysterious errand of her own, leaving me no choice but to request that the chairmen carry me once more.

I approached them with my usual smile, expecting the fawning obsequiousness that I had been told city servants possessed. Instead, I was shocked to see the amusement in his eyes as he denied my request.

"Sorry Miss Alison," the leading servant said, touching his hand to his forehead in a gesture that held much more of insolence than of subservience. "But Her Ladyship has expressly forbidden me from allowing you to use the sedan." I swear the rogue was grinning behind that bland face as he continued. "Her Ladyship said that you should walk, Miss Alison, for the exercise would be best for you."

Now, remember, my dears, Scottish servants are apt to think themselves your equal, no matter how lowly their station, so you must meet like for like.

"Thank you,"' I said to the oaf, determined not to let him see how irritated I was. "I shall follow Her Ladyship's advice and enjoy the walk."

"Yes Miss Alison," he replied. "And Her Ladyship said to remind you not to get lost, and not to plouter around in the mud more than you can help."

These servants really are more trouble than they are worth sometimes, especially if they have been with the family a long time. They are loyal as a Spartan of course but too familiar by half.

However, there was nothing for it but to walk and ignore the ill-concealed amusement of half the serving class of Edinburgh. You will remember how the Edinburgh New Town is cut off from the old by the great moat now filled by Princes Street Gardens. Imagine if you will, a great sheet of muddy water where the flower beds and lawns now are, fringe it with reeds and that was the North Loch. I had to walk down Hanover Street from Aunt Elspeth's town house in Queen Street, cross Princes Street and skirt the loch to the opposite shore. It was no great distance, but a bit fatiguing when one was fully figged out and preened to perfection.

I must have been a good twenty minutes on that short walk, trying to avoid the puddles, for it had rained during the night, and of course, I was splashed with mud by the time I reached the hut by the waterside.

Taking a deep breath and already forming my apology and my thanks, I rapped on the door, to find that there was no reply. For a moment I contemplated returning home, but I knew that Aunt Elspeth would check on me and probably send me back the next day, which would be galling in the extreme, and extremely fatiguing to my temper, so I opened the door and stepped inside, to be confronted by the shocking sight of an entirely naked man.

Chapter Four

My first reaction was to scream and withdraw, but curiosity forced me to linger an instant longer, for it was the first time I had seen a full grown man in nature's guise and the sight was quite delicious if shockingly scandalous. Believe me, my dears, most men are not worth the effort of even a single glance, yet alone a study, but Mr. Kemp was worth both, and more. I was fortunate that I had brothers, so I knew what shape and form males were, although it was many years since I had seen them in such a condition. Those years added much to a man, apparently, and I gave a little gasp.

It took that long for my presence to register with him and he started, covered the most disquieting parts of himself and turned aside. That was hardly an effective disguise, for it only afforded me a view of a different portion of his anatomy, and one which would be nearly as outrageous to the delicate eye.

"Mr. Kemp!" I said. "Pray cover yourself!"

He did try, placing one hand before and one behind, but the covering was still inadequate, so I thought it best to leave, but not, I hesitate to admit, without some reluctance and a last downward look.

I did bang the door, however, to make my discomfort obvious, and if I glanced back in case it did not close properly, I am sure that my action was inadvertent.

I heard various rustling noises and it was a good three minutes before Mr. Kemp appeared at his door, fully clad and with his dark hair dripping water down his face and onto the chest of his remarkably crisp linen shirt.

"Mr. Kemp," I said, trying not to let my eyes leave his face, or to be embarrassed by the full colour of my burning cheeks, "I should have knocked louder … I will say nothing of what I have just seen…"

"I cannot apologise enough," Mr. Kemp interrupted my intended apology. He looked as disconcerted as I had ever seen him, and still stood awkwardly as if a half crouch could erase the image of his person from my memory. "I had no idea that you were coming…"

"As I said, I will say nothing of what I have seen," I was determined to finish my piece and withdraw, so I could nurse my thoughts to myself and maybe share them with Louise once we had made up our ridiculous quarrel. We could have a fine time discussing things, now that I could match some of her stories with one of my own. And a true story at that, unlike her fantasies drawn from the pages of cheap novels.

"If I had known, I would certainly have been better dressed…" Mr. Kemp seemed intent on speaking through me in the most impolite manner.

"Indeed I will not mention it again. However, my aunt, Lady Elspeth Ballantyne, asked me if I would return…"

But that insolent man was still speaking as if I was only there to listen to him and his ridiculous excuses, and as if I cared if I had seen him naked or not. After all, he was only a mechanic. "As it is, I can only apologise for my state of undress and assure you that I had no intention of insulting you in any form at all…"

Ignoring his relentless talk, I continued. "Lady Elspeth Ballantyne asked me if I would return to apologise to you for my bad manners on the first of this month and to thank you…"

"So if you could see your way clear to forgiving me I would thank you…"

The coincidental use of an identical phrase struck us both simultaneously and we stopped together. For the first time, I properly looked at the man who stood opposite me.

Willie Kemp was as tall as I remembered, with that sensible length of hair and the side whiskers that extended no further than his ears, but now I noticed the steady brown eyes and the determined thrust of the jaw and the mouth that was lost somewhere between a plea for forgiveness and a smile of acceptance.

I curtsied, "Mr. Kemp," I said, finally completing the speech I had rehearsed on the weary road from the New Town. "I have come to beg forgiveness for my unwarrantable rudeness on my last visit, and to thank you for your kindness on that occasion."

Mr. Kemp bowed in return. "I assure you, Miss Lamont, that there is nothing to forgive and no need for thanks. I did no more than my Christian duty to a damsel in distress." When he straightened up he seemed to be looking at me with some curiosity. "But now I must ask your forgiveness for ... well, you know what for." It was then that he turned a most appealing tinge of pink, and I laughed out loud, which was perhaps not the most diplomatic of responses when standing in front of a man one had recently seen naked.

"Mr. Kemp," I stifled my laughter, which seemed to deepen his flush from pink to crimson. "I assure you that you have no reason at all to apologise. I did knock, but then I opened the door of your house without permission, and there can be no fault laid at your door for ... for whatever I saw."

We looked at each other again, neither of us quite sure what to say, but I felt that, as a gentlewoman, it was my place to take the lead. "Shall we put such misadventures behind us and start again?"

Mr. Kemp ducked his head in what I took to be graceful acknowledgement. "That would be best," he said and opened his door wide. "Would you care to enter? I can assure you that there are no unpleasant sights inside this time."

"There were no unpleasant sights last time, either," I thought, and the words were out of my mouth before I realised it. Luckily Mr. Kemp either did not hear or played the gentleman and made no reply, so once again I was inside his hut and sitting by that most welcoming fire.

I had not expected ever to return to Mr. Kemp's rustic abode, but once in, I was not surprised when he produced a bowl of fish and some silver cutlery that matched the brush and comb I had used on my previous visit. Perhaps he knew the thief, I thought, but the food was remarkably tasty, if simple, and the accompanying claret was of surprisingly good quality.

"So Mr. Kemp," I asked, "I have heard a number of most intriguing tales concerning your activities here. Pray tell me exactly what it is you do?"

I could not have chosen a better gambit to open a conversation. Whereas I suspected that talk of fashion or scandal or the French Wars would have left him cold, those few words opened a golden doorway that I found it nearly impossible to close. Mr. Kemp's face, normally so sombre and controlled, lit up with an animation such as I had seldom seen in a man, and never in a woman unless it was on Louise when she was discussing a new dress or a fanciful romantic encounter.

"I am an engineer," he told me, and before I could make any further enquiry, he explained exactly what he engineered, and how, and with what materials, and to what end. Indeed, before that hour was completed I heard more about engineering than I ever had in my life and far more than interested me. In saying that, it is always fascinating to listen to somebody who knows his subject, so I must have learned something.

At that period, my dears, the country was not crisscrossed with railway tracks and covered with steam powered factories as it is now. If you wanted to travel, you jumped in a coach, or rode a horse, or used a sedan chair for shorter journeys. Some people even walked wherever they wanted to go, and the sea was covered in sail-powered ships. Honestly, my dears, you can have no concept of just how many sailing vessels there were; every port, every harbour, every little creek had its quota, and if you visited the coast there was nothing to see but ships and boats of every description. The French ogre Bonaparte had tried to stop our maritime trade, but he may as well have tried to Canute the tide. But apparently, this was not good enough for Mr. Kemp.

"You see, Miss Lamont," he told me, all bright- eyed enthusiasm and zestful for progress, "sailing ships cannot sail against the wind!"

"I know that," I said, proud of my learning.

He ignored my youthful sarcasm. "So if the wind is in the wrong quarter, they are all stormbound, sitting idly at anchor and wasting time and money while valuable cargoes rot."

I nodded. "That is just a fact of life," I said. "It is something that is always with us, like the poor or lawyers."

"Not necessarily," Mr. Kemp said, and then he was off. I have never heard a man as enthusiastic as he described his plan for creating a vessel that could sail at any time, whatever the state of wind or tide, powered entirely by steam. "Some people have tried it before," he said, "but only ever in inland waterways, the Forth and Clyde Canal, say, but I want to see a whole fleet of seagoing steam ships."

I listened for some time as the morning eased past. "These seagoing steam boats," I said at last, in an attempt to stem the rush of words, "will they actually work? Will they not just catch fire?"

My question only made him more animated, if anything. He began to speak of boilers and rotating paddles and connecting rods and steam pressure and other mechanical babble that could mean nothing to any civilised person until I finally yelled at him to stop.

"What?" He said, looking all bemused and hurt.

I eased his hurt with my most amiable smile. "I am only a woman," I reminded, playing on my feminine wiles for probably the first time. We can all do that, you know, my dears. You will practise on your father, for what daughter cannot wind a loving father around her little finger with a smile and a wide-eyed look, but it works even better with a man who has not known you since birth. It is the best weapon in our arsenal, the coy smile, the flick of the hair, the look of bemusement when you want them to close their mouths for a few precious minutes.

It certainly worked on Willie Kemp that day, for rather than ex- plaining every detail of his devices, he said that he would show me.

"Show me?" I must have squawked in his ear. "Do you mean that you have actually constructed one of these devilish things?"

"I most certainly have." He looked surprised at my question as if everybody spent their life trying to make things that worked against God's own nature.

Before I quite understood what was happening, he was conducting me to a long wooden shed that stood a few yards from his own and which was concealed from the casual walker by a hedge of brambles and such like entangling vegetation. I was glad that I had not donned my best clothes for such a visitation but resolved never again to pretty my face before meeting Mr. Willie Kemp. Not, of course, that I had any intention of doing any such thing.

Mr. Kemp seemed to be trembling as he hauled open the door of this second shed, and he lit a series of lanterns that illuminated the interior most elegantly.

"Well then," he said. "What do you think of her?"

I looked and shook my head. It was like nothing that I had ever seen before. Indeed I suspected that nobody had ever seen the like. Sitting on a sort of wooden trestle was a weird contraption with the hull of a boat, but rather than a mast, a great cylindrical chimney, for the entire world like a top hat, thrust up to the wooden ceiling. Behind this chimney was a great metal box, apparently called a boiler, and connecting the two was a mass of pipes and levers and metal bits and pieces the function of I could only guess.

At the back of the hull was a huge wheel, with flat bits of wood set at right angles to the circumference.

"What on earth," I began, and then I looked at Mr. Kemp's face.

It was then that I fell in love with him. By now you must have guessed that was going to happen, or I would not have spent so much time on his ridiculous foibles, but it was when he looked on his creation and I saw the expression of total devotion on his face that I realised here was a man with a passion that did not begin, centre and end entirely on himself, or on hunting and shooting. Suddenly I wanted a man to look at me with the same rapturous expression as he did with his mechanical devices, and not just any man, but this man, this dirty-fingered Willie Kemp.

Now I can hear your thoughts already, although I am probably long gone and you may never even meet me or at least in my dribbling dotage. A mechanic, you are thinking. How on earth can a gentle woman fall in love with a mechanic, how can you cross the great divide of culture and class and position and money? Well, let me tell you ladies, that when you experience love, such things do not matter; it happens, you can do nothing about it and that is that.

So I was in love. I did not quite know it yet, but the seed was well and truly planted, and all it needed was fertile soil and a decent watering of opportunity. How we would live, of course, I had no idea, for I had no intention of spending the remainder of my life in a shed beside a muddy loch. But we cannot tell the future, thank the Lord, and all things are revealed in time.

"What do you think?" Mr. Kemp asked with that expression of adoration on his face, and I had not the heart to tell him that it was the most ridiculous looking contraption in God's creation.

"It's beautiful," I said, and that was the first lie that I ever told him. Now lying is an art, dears. You must never lie about anything important, and you must never lie to hurt, but to keep a marriage or a man it is sometimes better to lie than to be brutally honest. Men are fragile things, you see, and bruise easily, so one must constantly smooth their lives with praise. I tell you these things so your own lives can be easier and you can control your own marriages, and not because I want you to lie all the time. You lie only when you must and never to your great-grandmother or she will lace you so you needs sleep on your face.

"Do you think so?"

I nodded enthusiastically, all the time wishing that I was somewhere else, to examine the plethora of mixed feelings that I had never experienced before. Love is like that also, you see, it is a powerful emotion that can sometimes be difficult to handle. Better in small doses at first, until you are used to it, and then it takes over and you are under its influence in whatever you do. There is no help for it, my dears, for it as powerful a drug as religion or laudanum.

"Does it work?" I asked foolishly.

"I don't know yet," he said, with surprising honesty for a man. You see men always exaggerate their own capabilities and attributes. They do that in every capacity, my dears, so do not be disappointed when the crucial moment arrives.

"Oh," I said as if I were disappointed.

"But we can try her out," he said, and there was such excitement in his voice that I knew I could not hurt him. I also noticed, with some dismay, his use of the inclusive 'we' so I was involved in whatever he had planned.

Being quite a skilled engineer, and no mere mechanic, Mr. Kemp had rigged wheels onto the wooden trestle and had created a roadway so the whole contraption could be run from the shed into the loch. I expected there to be a great deal of huffing and muscle wrenching, but instead, it ran smoothly as any custom-built coach.

Within twenty minutes Mr. Kemp had opened two great doors at the loch end of the hut and had wheeled the trestle and its ugly boat into the water, where it floated in an ungainly, but apparently safe, fashion.

"There we go," Mr. Kemp grinned at me, still with that animated brightness in his eyes. "Would you care to join me?"

I would have much preferred to remain safely on land, even when the mud was again threatening to ruin my boots, but somehow I found myself clambering over the low gunwale and standing inside that weird contraption. I could feel the boat rocking from side to side, and immediately regretted my action, but naturally I would not admit to my fears.

"You just sit there," Mr. Kemp said, "while I get up steam."

There were three seats, or rather benches, set in front of that great circular wheel in the stern, that's the back end of the boat, and I perched as gently as I could in case the thing should turn over and drown us both.

Mr. Kemp had no such qualms, for he bustled about with coal and shovels, lighting a fire, which seemed an immensely dangerous procedure on board a boat, and doing things with levers and rods that I did not understand then and still do not understand now. However, whatever he did must have been effective, for the engine began to make strange sounds, dirty smoke eased from the chimney, or funnel as Mr. Kemp called it, the great circular wheel began to turn around and within the hour we were moving.

I gave a little scream and held onto my bonnet, but I need not have worried for I could have walked far faster than that boat sailed. The wheel or paddle wheel as it was, moved about a dozen times, just enough to propel us into the centre of the loch, and then stopped.

Mr. Kemp said a very ungentlemanly word.

"Mr. Kemp!" I said, pretending to be shocked but actually quite enjoying this display of genuine emotion from a man who on our first meeting had appeared so guarded.

He apologised at once for he was genuinely contrite at having sullied my innocent ears with such foul language. Men have a strange idea of women; perhaps they think we live within a glass bottle and only come out on their invitation, like some eastern genie. However, I accepted his apology and asked whatever could be the matter and why ever have we stopped? Perhaps we have reached our destination?

"Oh no," Mr. Kemp explained, quite concerned that I should be aware of every movement of his machine. "The connecting rod has disconnected."

"Can you replace it?" I asked sweetly, while the wind played on our boat and a few passersby on Princes Street stopped to watch. I toyed with the notion of waving playfully to them but thought it beneath the dignity of a lady.

"I can try," Mr. Kemp said, and he dived head first into his machine, clattering and banging with a variety of tools and making the very devil of a din that must surely have scared the horses for half a mile in every direction.

It took another half hour to get the boat moving again, and we both cheered when the paddle wheels began their circuits, churning up the water to a creamy brown froth and pushing the boat crab wise. Notice I said crab-wise, not forward or in reverse, for we skidded back and forth across that infernal loch all morning, with Mr. Kemp tinkering with his engine and half the population of Edinburgh lining Princes Street to mock our progress. I swear that I used up my stock of patience long before noon, and I had enough of Mr. Kemp's excuses and promised that "just one more turn" of some tool or another would sort out all the problems in the world.

"Mr. Kemp," I said at length, "please take me back."

"Are you not enjoying yourself?" He seemed genuinely amazed that I was not in raptures when sitting in a freezing boat in the middle of a loch in January while half the population of Edinburgh gawped at us.

"I would rather be back on dry land," I said, as tactfully as possible.

To give him his due, Mr. Kemp did turn his boat around and returned me to the wooden trestle, and he jumped into the water without a qualm and hauled the thing back inside without asking for any assistance. Of course, I watched, and when it was obvious that he was struggling I could not help but slid into the water and push the infernal thing up the ramp.

"That was how I got so wet this morning," he told me, as the water again dripped from his face.

"I can imagine," I replied, although I had not totally immersed myself and was wet only up to my poor knees.

He began to laugh, and I had to join in and we both stood there in that wooden shed, laughing together while the boat dripped water and a long sliver of weed was wrapped around my left leg.

"We'll have to get you warm again," he said, "you're shivering there."

"Yes," I said and, leaning forward, I kissed him.

That was the first time that I ever kissed a man, save for duty kisses in the family, and it was probably the strangest experience in my life. I do not know what made me do it, save for the turmoil of emotions within me, but it surprised me nearly as much as it did Willie Kemp.

It was not a long kiss, but pleasant, but he recoiled after just a couple of seconds, staring at me in something that I took to be horror.

"Miss Lamont," he said, with one hand on his mouth and the other holding on to his boat for support.

"Oh my Lord," I felt myself colour up. "Oh my Lord, Mr. Kemp, I do apologise, I really do; I should not have done such a thing…"

"No," he stepped back slightly and for a moment I wondered if he was going to walk out of the shed and into the loch in his desire to escape from such a forward miss as I was proving to be. And I had blamed Louise for such behaviour only the previous day; what a lot I understood now, and what a lot we had to talk about that night. I felt a feeling of warm affection for my misunderstood cousin.

"No," Mr. Kemp repeated. "You should not have done such a thing." He moved slightly closer. "I should have."

If my kiss had been only slightly more than a peck, then Mr. Kemp's was something far more substantial, and far longer lasting. Without touching any part of me other than my mouth, he bent over me and kissed me soundly. I did not resist, my dears, for I wanted nothing else and nobody else. I had felt the first pangs of love before our loch voyage, but now it was confirmed. It deepened and strengthened during those few moments, or was it an hour or an eternity?

Some things are timeless, my dears, and some memories deserve to last forever, and that kiss was one such. Although only our lips met, it was if our souls merged together and we were indeed one, although there was nothing physical and no promises made or accepted.

I just knew, as simply and surely as I know that God is in heaven or the stars are far away. I had neither proof nor need of proof, I just knew, and that knowledge was so solid that nothing else was needed.

Damn you, Willie Kemp, for tying my heart in so secure a knot, and bless you, Willie Kemp, for that day on the loch. It is a treasure of a memory, one that shines in a filament of laughter, and one I needed in the days to come, as you will hear by and by if you have read this far, my dear ones.

"I have wanted to do that since you first stepped into my life, dripping wet and defiant," Willie Kemp said, and he was smiling down at me.

"Oh," I said, for I could think of nothing more sensible to say. You see, I thought that all the feelings were on my side and that I had seized and held the initiative. I had not thought that a mere mechanic, or even an engineer, would dare have feelings for a lady born and bred.

"Shall we try again?" He asked.

I may have hesitated, for a thousand thoughts were swirling around my head, a thousand images and a thousand ideas, from the foolish notion of marriage to this fellow to wondering what Aunt Elspeth would say, to the constantly recurring memory of Mr. Kemp as I had first seen him that day. I say that I may have hesitated, and I certainly coloured up, but neither prevented me from meeting his kiss with one more passionate than before and this time we held each other in busy hands.

"My aunt Elspeth will never approve of this," I said when we broke for breath.

"Your aunt Elspeth does not know," Mr. Kemp reminded, with a deep twinkle in those brown eyes.

"I might tell her," I warned.

"So might I," he retorted, and I knew that neither of us would break the secret of this day, for I trusted Willie Kemp.

Fool that I was, for no man ever tells a woman everything about himself, and Mr. William Kemp had more secrets than a household of women, and maybe I was only the least of them. But I did not know that, then, you see, and I only believed what seemed to be true.

We broke after the fourth or perhaps the fifth kiss and Mr. Kemp stepped back, still smiling with his eyes, although his lips were strong and serene, if perhaps slightly swollen. As were my own of course, and I hoped that Louise did not pry too closely what I had been up to, to return with my lips afire and my eyes no doubt as bright as a summer morning.

"You must go back to your aunt," Mr. Kemp told me, but I shook my head.

"Not yet," I said, "please, not yet."

"You must," he said, and there was desperation in his face that I did not understand, for I did not know him then or men. He was honourable in his own way, was Mr. Kemp, and he was attempting to save me from what might have seemed an inevitable conclusion to our behaviour.

And what of me? I was too young to know and too foolish to care.

"Just a few minutes more," I pleaded, and he relented, allowing one last fond kiss, as the poet says, and then he made me dry the end of my skirt at his constantly-burning fire. Disappearing into the small room, he changed himself into the clothes that I had been wearing, which made me smile at the smallness of his wardrobe and readied himself to escort me home.

"You cannot come," I told him, rather pointedly and extremely rudely.

"I think I had better," he said. "It's not right for a lady to walk alone, not after that riot the other night. Indeed, I am surprised that your aunt sent you by yourself."

So I was escorted back from that significant little hut, along Princes Street and into the New Town. I felt strange, walking with a man who was so obviously my social inferior, but who carried himself with all the confidence of a lord or a successful merchant. There were a few raised eyebrows, but as they came from people that I did not know, it did not matter, and in some perverse way it felt quite good to have such a large and powerful man walking at my side. At least I knew that none of the Edinburgh cowlies, for such was that city's name for a footpad or rogue, would dare accost me with Willie Kemp there.

He was sensible enough to leave me at the corner of Queen Street and Hanover Street, and although I half- suspected that he wanted to steal one last kiss, he did not ask, which was slightly disappointing. I wanted to desperately to turn around and see if he watched me all the way, but such an action was beneath my dignity, so I forbore. I still do not know.

I walked into the great hallway of Aunt Elspeth's Queen Street townhouse, with the arched window above the door allowing in light and the painting of some battle or other wasting most of the space in the inner wall. My heart was singing, all was well with the world and I could think of nothing except Willie Kemp. I thought of his mannerisms and the tone of his voice, of the touch of his hands on my shoulders and the way his eyes softened when he smiled. I recalled other images also, but I will not go into that here, my dears, and I will allow you to give free play to your imaginations.

Aunt Elspeth descended the stairs exactly as I entered, with her cream and gold dress as serene as always and her hair immaculate to a fault. Not that Aunt Elspeth would ever admit to a fault.

"Ah, Miss Alison."

"Yes Aunt Elspeth," I said, and wondered if I should tell her about Mr. Kemp right away, or impart the good news during our evening meal. I was desperate to tell somebody, and Louise did not seem to be around. I was hardly aware of the sodden state of my lower skirt, and, strangely, my severe aunt also failed to notice my appearance.

"I have some news for you, dear. Some very good news." Aunt Elspeth seemed to have quite forgiven me for my actions at Lady Catriona's ball.

I smiled, waiting to for the day to get even better.

"Come into the withdrawing room, Miss Alison, and sit down."

I knew by now that all the important business was conducted in the withdrawing room, from announcements of forthcoming balls to family business and even the occasional small rebuke. I followed my aunt, wishing that I had dried the foot of my dress at Mr. Kemp's fire and smiling at some of the images that recurred. Would Louise not be green with jealousy when I told her of my adventures?

"Sit down, Alison."

I perched on the sofa, in exactly the same position as Louise had taken only two days previously. The clock was still ticking softly and the sounds of the street were subdued in the late afternoon. The light was already beginning to fade, I noticed, so the servants would build up the fire ready for a warm evening in the house.

"Well Alison, you are aware that your mother sent you to Edinburgh in the hope that you might find a suitable husband. Good men are so scarce in the Highlands these days, what with every really eligible young man joining the army as soon as he can hold a musket."

"Yes, Aunt Elspeth," I said, keeping my head down and my secret to myself.

"Well, I am glad to say that I have already found the most suitable man for you."

I looked up at that, wondering how Aunt Elspeth could have spoken to Mr. Kemp so quickly.

"And I have found a man who has already made his feelings for you quite clear."

It was Willie Kemp. They must have spoken even before Aunt Elspeth sent me to his hut. No wonder Mr. Kemp told me that he had wanted to kiss me from the moment we met. It was all cut and dried.

"I think that you know exactly who I mean," Aunt Elspeth said, and I nodded.

"Yes, Aunt Elspeth, and I could not be happier!"

"Good! Then that is settled then. As soon as it can be arranged, you will become Mrs. John Forres."

Chapter Five

I sat, completely stunned, staring at Aunt Elspeth. I could not believe how wrong she was. Only a few seconds before I had been dreaming of a life with Willie Kemp, that large and honourable, if poor and eccentric man, and now she had told me I was to marry the dandified John Forres, a creature with the smoothest of tongues and the slyest of eyes.

"No," I said. "You cannot mean it!"

Taking my exclamation for joyous disbelief, Lady Elspeth smiled and nodded.

"Oh, I do Alison. As soon as I heard that he admired you at Lady Caroline's Hogmanay Ball, I knew that he was just the husband for you. Imagine; you will be married into one of the largest landowning families in the Highlands, your own part of the world. When Mr. Alexander Forres dies, Mr. John Forres will have an income of some £20,000 a year. Imagine!" And she sat there, looking like the cat who has found a mouse hidden in its cream, the obtuse old harridan. I say old, but she was not old at all, but at that time I thought she was positively ancient.

I was unsure what was best to do. Should I begin to bawl my eyes out, or keep a stiff and polite silence, or beg her to reconsider?

"I realise that this news must be overwhelming," Aunt Elspeth said, perhaps with some kindly intent, "so it may be best if you were to withdraw to your room and consider the possibilities of your new life." She stood up and held out her hand as if she were a Queen awaiting a kiss from a flattered commoner. "Tomorrow we will take the carriage to the Forres Residence and make the formalities."

"Tomorrow?" I stared at my aunt.

"There is no point in delaying such things. So repair to your room now, and compose yourself."

I obliged of course. It is always best to remain in the favour of the royals. Besides which, I did not know what to say.

"Well, Miss Alison," Aunt Elspeth called out to me as I negotiated the stairs, "that's your future assured, and so soon after your arrival in Edinburgh. I hope that you are as pleased with yourself as I am."

Have you heard the expression about your heart sinking into your shoes? Well, that is exactly how mine felt. Tomorrow was very close.

John Forres. The name haunted me as I slouched up the stairs that led to my shared bedroom. John Forres, that smooth- mannered, perfumed mountebank. What on earth had Aunt Elspeth in mind when she selected him?

Throwing open the door, I threw myself down on the bed, buried my face in my pillow and began to howl. It was quite some time before I realised that I was not alone. Louise was lying in exactly the same position on her bed, giving vent to her feelings in exactly the same way.

I looked over to her for a few minutes, noting how undignified a woman is when face down on her bed with her shoulders heaving and her bottom wobbling with emotion. Did I look like that? I must have, and the thought was not pretty. What would Mr. Kemp think of me now?

I watched as Louise lifted her head, took a deep breath and began another bout of grief- stricken yells that must surely have been held in the street outside, yet alone down stairs by Aunt Elspeth and the others in the household.

"What on earth is wrong with you?" I asked, nearly forgetting my horror at being paired with John Forres. After all, I was young, and such an event was somewhere in the future, not an immediate happening. The young have a way of putting tomorrow off in the expectation that it never happens. That way leads only to heartache, dears, so make sure that you grasp your future firmly in both your own hands, rather than allowing others to direct it for you.

Louise looked up, her pretty face interestingly swollen by tears and her eyes puffy and red. "Mother is marrying you to John Forres," she wailed, slobbering all over herself, "and it's not fair. I should be marrying him."

I allowed her to return to her sodden pillow while I lay back. For a few moments, I wondered about John Forres. True it would be delightful to be mistress of £20,000 a year, so there would be no more scrimping and saving, no more worrying about household expenses, and my children, and I was fully determined to have a whole brood of girls and boys, would be most carefully brought up.

And then I thought of Willie Kemp's kindness and his enthusiasm over that ridiculous boat, and the way he looked after me that night. I thought of other things related to Mr. Kemp too, but they are not for your ears or eyes, my dears. Find your own man and do not peep into the intimacies I shared with one I fondly hoped would be mine, fool that I was.

There was no comparison. I honestly believed that Mr. Kemp and I had chosen each other, while Aunt Elspeth had foisted John Forres onto me.

"Louise," I said, but she was too intent on sobbing to hear me.

I tried again. "Louise!"

She looked round slowly. "Go away," she said. "I hate you."

"I hate you too," I told her pleasantly, "but that does not really matter just now. You see, I don't want John Forres at all."

Louise's look could have melted cheese. "I don't care what you want. I only care what I want, and I want John Forres for myself!"

That really confirmed my opinion of Miss Louise but did nothing to help me. I could feel the tears returning to my eyes as I thought of the future that Aunt Elspeth had planned for me. Was there anything I could do to escape?

I did not know.

And that thought kept me awake for most of the night as I listened to Louise sobbing and snuffling and I thought about the happenings of the day.

Lady Catriona was not effusive in her welcome when Aunt Elspeth brought me back to the Forres residence. She looked at me as if I had crawled from beneath some stone but treated me politely for the sake of my aunt.

"So this is the young lady that so interested my grandson." Her eyes were shrewd as she surveyed me. "There's quite a lot of you," she said pointedly and I felt myself colouring up.

To explain, Lady Catriona was little more than a wraith, a woman who had kept her lack of shape while generations had grown past her. I was not quite so slender, but curves were in fashion in 1812, you see, and we were not afraid to eat.

"Yes, Lady Catriona," I said.

She probed me for a long moment. "I had to ask you to leave my Hogmanay Ball, Miss Lamont."

I agreed again, hoping that she would see fit to ban me from her family as effectively as she had banished me from her house.

"Well," she said, suddenly smiling, "I am sure that we can put that behind us, now that we know the truth of the matter." She stood up from the chair to which she seemed to have been rooted for some time. "John told me what really happened, so it appears that you hold a genuine appeal for him."

Lady Catriona began to circle me, like a cat stalking some defenceless bird. Although she had changed her gown for something so comfortable that it seemed a shapeless blanket of a creation, her turban remained the same. "Perhaps there is something there, after all, Miss Lamont. Perhaps there is something other than your wild Highland ways."

Unsure what to say, I said nothing and allowed her scrutiny to continue.

"So this is Miss Alison Lamont is it?" I had not noticed that there were two other women in the room. One was young and handsome, with auburn hair and a strong face. The other woman was older and sat half hidden behind the pianoforte. She emerged now and looked at me in a manner every bit as direct as that of Lady Catriona. 'From Badenoch, I believe?"

"Yes, ma'am," I waited hopefully for an introduction.

"Mrs. Anne Cairnsmuir," Aunt Elspeth told me.

"And you are to be married to Mr. John Forres?" Mrs. Cairnsmuir continued as if my aunt had never spoken.

I nodded as the stark truth returned to me. I was to spend the remainder of my life chained to a man that I despised. The sheer horror of that sentence struck me anew.

"I believe that the two of you met only on Hogmanay?" Mrs. Cairnsmuir asked. "It is so short a time for such a deep commitment." She looked at me quizzically. "But sometimes one needs only a few moments, I believe."

Thinking of Mr. Kemp, I agreed.

"Then perhaps things are already decided," Mrs. Cairnsmuir said slowly.

The tears were hot behind my eyes.

"So greet your intended, Miss Lamont." Lady Catriona ordered and watched to ensure I was standing correctly or perhaps that my curtsey was low enough when the lucky man stepped in.

Mr. John Forres looked exactly as he had on the night of the ball. He was tall and smart, with that scarlet uniform like a badge of honour and a smile stretching his glossy, immaculately shaved skin.

"My dear Miss Lamont; I am so pleased that we are to be united in marriage," his bow was so low that his head nearly bobbed from his mother's Axminster carpet.

"Mister Forres," wishing I was anywhere but in the Forres Residence, I gave the briefest of curtsies. When I straightened up, Mrs. Cairnsmuir was watching closely, with a small frown on her face.

"Good," Lady Elspeth said. "Now that we have agreed upon the union, we can make the arrangements as quickly as possible. There is no need to delay such an event. Your grandson John requires a wife,

and my niece will be better with a husband to curb her waywardness."
Her nod was as good as the full stop that ends a solicitor's letter.

"Waywardness?" Mrs. Cairnsmuir stepped forward. "As the god-
mother of John Forres, I believe that it is in my interest to know the
details."

I had wondered what her position was, and why she was present at
what should be a family affair.

"My niece is quick- tempered," Lady Elspeth said evenly, "and she is
apt to impulsiveness." Her smile was full of irony. "I can add a distorted
sense of direction to her faults, and sometimes a lack of judgement."

"Impulsiveness is natural for somebody of her age," Mrs. Cairnsmuir
said, "as is a quick temper. Maturity will cure both."

Good advice my dears, but completely false, of course, for I am as
impulsive as I ever was, and if you want an example of my temper,
then cross me, once. But Mrs. Cairnsmuir, God rest her bones, was not
to know that away back in 1812.

"As for a distorted sense of direction, well, that may be an asset,
given the correct circumstances. However, a lack of judgement could
be serious. Tell me, Miss Lamont," surprisingly, Mrs. Cairnsmuir addressed me directly, rather than speaking as if I were only an object
to be discussed. I began to like her a little better. "In what manner did
this fault become apparent?"

"I am not quite sure what my aunt means," I replied cautiously. "Perhaps it would be better to ask her."

"Miss Lamont is quite aware what I meant," Aunt Elspeth said hotly.
"She lost herself on the journey from this residence the other night
and…"

"I see," Mrs. Cairnsmuir nodded. "I have indeed heard that story."
She looked at me, and then at John Forres. "And what does Mr. Forres
think about it?"

John Forres was surreptitiously engaged in admiring his silhouette
in a mirror. As I watched he placed two fingers inside an inside pocket
and produced a snuff box in the shape of a woman's leg. Still watching
himself, he practised opening it with an apparently casual flick of his

left thumb, removed a pinch and thrust it up each nostril in turn. His sneeze was as elegant as any could be, and only then did he return his attention to us.

"I do beg your pardon, ladies, were you addressing me?" He indicated his box. "Belongaro, don't you know. One of the finest snuffs ever made."

I hoped that Mrs. Cairnsmuir would allow the matter to drop, but she seemed determined to embarrass me. "I asked what you thought about your intended's behaviour the other night."

"Simply appalling," he said. "She should be thoroughly ashamed of herself." He fixed me with what he thought was a stern glare. "Miss Lamont requires a good man to keep her in line, and I'm just the fellow."

"Just the fellow," Mrs. Cairnsmuir repeated.

I had remained demure until then, but as I opened my mouth to give my opinion, Lady Catriona rang a little handbell and a liveried servant brought in a tray of drinks. There was orgeat for me, probably the safest and least powerful drink known to man, or woman, no doubt in case I fell down again, or ran off with the footman or started to sing a republican song, while the ladies could imbibe claret, and Lady Catriona slurped down a tumbler full of the finest Ferintosh. For somebody who claimed to despise my wild Highland ways, she made short work of the whisky.

"So you have no objection to your intended spending the night at a man's house and with no female chaperone?" Mrs. Cairnsmuir seemed to be labouring the point.

"There is no harm done, apparently," John Forres sipped at his claret. "It seems that the gentleman in question did not take advantage of the opportunity thus presented." He looked at me with a smile. "Of course, once you are mine, my dear, I expect you to act with more circumspection."

I swallowed hard, feeling frustrated tears rise to my eyes. Should I meekly agree? Or give vent to my true feelings. "Of course, Mr. Forres."

"You know that your duty as a wife is to provide one healthy male heir. After that, you are free to amuse yourself as you please, as long as it does not involve me in a scandal. I have no desire to wear the cuckold's horns." His laugh was light. "Conduct your affairs with discretion madam, and I will not embarrass you with mine."

So my dears, you see that my intended had no intention of being a faithful husband. I might have expected the ladies present to look scandalised at this display of John Forres' moral philosophy, but none of them turned a hair. My generation was the most dreadful hypocrites, you see, where adultery was accepted, but scandal was not. John was merely voicing what was common practice. He was a man of his times, and honest in his own way.

Now I am not asking you to emulate our behaviour, my dears, for we have moved on since my time, and this Queen Victoria has installed much higher standards in the country. However, we all live according to the lights current in our formative youth, I believe and treat all other values with disdain.

I stood beside Mr. John Forres for quite ten minutes, waiting for him to say something of the slightest interest, but save for some casual comments about the weather; his conversation was of fashion and high society.

"Not that I would expect you to know these people, dear Miss Alison," he said most condescendingly, "but when we are married you will be moving in the most exalted company and it is best to be able to fit in, don't you know?"

I nodded and attempted to look demure. "Yes, Mr. Forres," I agreed. I could see the other ladies nodding their approval. To them, it seemed obvious that John Forres would lead me in the correct manner. I would be the dutiful wife, attending the correct parties and meeting only those of our own social standing.

William Kemp and that small hut by the loch began to drift further away. I wondered how his steam boat was today, and if he had managed to steer it in a straight line yet. Somehow I doubted it.

"And as for the servants," John Forres was teaching me how to manage a house, now. "You must treat them with a firm hand, dear Miss Lamont, and never allow them to take over. They will cheat you from morning until Christmas, given half a chance, you know." He looked at me, "indeed perhaps I should check over your household accounts every month. I was fairly good at mathematics."

"He was indeed," Lady Catriona nodded to support her grandson. "He was far from the bottom of the class."

And equally far from the top, I wagered, wondering who he bribed or coerced into doing his prep for him.

The remainder of the day passed in equally exciting conversation, but I will refrain from including you in my exquisite boredom. Suffice to say that by the time I left the Forres Residence I knew that I would never marry John Forres, however much my aunt, Lady Caroline, Mrs. Cairnsmuir and Uncle Tom Cobley and all tried to persuade me. Actually, Mrs. Cairnsmuir did not try very hard, but asked a great many difficult questions and generally acted as Devil's advocate, which was just as bad.

Louise was not interested in my complaints, being far more concerned with her own shattered dreams. However, she was no longer engaged in washing the pillow with her tears and had time to scream her hatred of me.

I allowed her to vent her feelings for a few minutes.

"Besides, I have a new beau now. You can keep Mr. John Forres."

I shook my head, "but I don't want him," I said.

Louise's scream must have been heard right along Queen Street. "You don't want him and I do," she said and began a new bout of sobbing that kept me awake half that night. As I lay there with the pillow muffling the sounds, I planned how best to escape from this intolerable position in which I found myself.

Chapter Six

Willie Kemp stared at me over the intricate metal structure that he was adding to his steam boat. "You want what?"

I repeated my words, stuttering when I realised the enormity of my request. "I want you to help me."

Ushering me to the seat, he stood by the fire, sighing as if in deep thought. "Let me get this straight, Miss Lamont." His voice was grave and deep, a schoolmaster lecturing his pupils rather than a man speaking to a woman who loved him. "Your aunt has ordered that you marry John Forres."

"That is correct," I heard the tremble in my voice.

"In doing so, your aunt is merely complying with your mother's request."

I nodded. My mother had indeed sent me down to Edinburgh with a plea for Aunt Elspeth to find a husband.

"And as you are a minor you are obliged to obey both your mother and your aunt."

Again I nodded. I could not argue with Mr. Kemp's logic, and I began to hate him too. I felt completely alone in this city and wished desperately that I was home amongst my own hills. I knew that I did not belong in this grey place of regular streets and cold, mechanical people.

"So far then, Miss Lamont, you have no reason to complain," said this man that I had run to for comfort. "Now tell me, would this be a favourable marriage? Is Mr. Forres a wealthy man?"

"He is," I said stiffly. I had not expected such an interrogation and felt my lip thrust out sulkily. Lord, but I could be a sulky puss when I wanted to, me that thought of myself as so re

"So no complaints there either." Mr. Kemp said. "So I fail to see why you are unhappy with this proposed match, Miss Lamont." He gave a faint but infuriating smile. "Does he have two heads, perhaps? Or is he misshapen in some other way?"

I shook my head once more. "Indeed he is a handsome enough fellow, and quite well favoured about his person as far as I can see."

"So as Dr. Pangloss would say, 'all is for the best in this best of all possible lives.'"

I felt like stamping my foot in frustration if it would not have seemed so childlike. "But I don't like the man!"

"So your only objection is that you are not in love with him," Mr. Kemp eventually came to what was really the crux of the matter.

"Exactly," I agreed, pleased that Mr. Kemp, at last, appeared to agree with me. I was wrong of course.

"You do realise that most fashionable marriages are arranged in such manner, and the participants usually manage to jog along tolerably well. Your marriage will be no exception, and most people will wonder why you are making such a fuss." When he looked down at me with his eyebrows raised in that fashion I hated him all the more.

I do not know if I have ever felt more wretched than I did at that moment. I had left Aunt Elspeth's house and run to Mr. Kemp's for support and comfort, but instead, he had torn my argument to shreds and obviously thought that I should comply with Aunt Elspeth's orders.

"But I do not love him," I wailed, completely forgetting in my misery to appear refined and dignified. Really, my dears, deep emotion can be a terrible thing. Sometimes it is far better to live life on the surface. But on other occasions, the rewards can be far greater if you explore your deeper feelings, it all depends on your personality, I presume.

"Does that matter?" Mr. Kemp continued, cruelly ignoring my distress.

"Yes!" This time I did stamp my foot as I glared at him hotly.

"Why?" That single word made me stop dead.

Why did it matter? I was being offered everything that a young woman could desire. If I married John Forres, I would be mistress of a large property, with sufficient income to ensure that I wanted for nothing in my life. Mr. Forres had already made it clear that he would not be a demanding husband, quite satisfied with a single heir. But I did not want Mr. Forres.

"Mr. Kemp," I kept my voice as calm as I could. "I will not marry Mr. Forres, never in the reign of Queen Dick."

Mr. Kemp sank down until he squatted right beside me with his face so serious that I knew his next question would be crucial. His words were straight to the point. "Why not?"

"Because I love somebody else," I told him and hoped that he would ask who that person might be. After our quite passionate kissing on our previous encounter, I thought the answer was obvious, but I had yet to learn that men are obtuse about such matters. Their view of relationships is quite different from ours.

"Ah," Mr. Kemp looked away. "And does this fortunate fellow also love you?"

I looked into those deep brown eyes and told the entire truth. "I don't know," I said, hopelessly. "I have not asked him." The tears came back then, and it seemed natural to drop my head on Willie Kemp's shoulder and natural for him to put a strong arm around me.

"Then you do need somebody to help you," Mr. Kemp said kindly, "until you find the courage to ask."

"Thank you," I said humbly, putting my trust in the kindness of this mechanic. It was obvious that he liked me, but that was all, so how could I say that it was him I loved when we were from two such different backgrounds? A man like Willie Kemp would be utterly dismayed to hear that a lady could love him, for he could never give her the life style that she desired.

"Can I stay here for a while?" I knew at once that the question was unanswerable. If Mr. Kemp agreed he would be putting himself to great inconvenience, for at that age I did not understand the economics of food and shelter. I had no idea how much it cost to feed and clothe somebody, to say nothing of winter fuel, for such things had always appeared magically for me. We were indeed a spoiled generation, my dears, and it is little wonder that so many of our class lived far beyond our means.

Mr. Kemp continued to look at me with that half smile on his face and his eyes deep brown. "Does Lady Elspeth know that you are here?"

"Of course not!" I refuted the suggestion immediately. "I told my aunt that I was going for a walk to mull things over. She has no idea that I am here."

Mr. Kemp nodded. "I see. Well, even so, I do not think it is best for you to live with me."

I nearly burst into tears at the disappointment. I really believed that Willie Kemp would have been able to take me in, somehow and look after me as he had on Hogmanay. "But what will I do?' Where will I go?" I was becoming frantic now. "I can't marry that man!"

Mr. Kemp sighed with infinite patience. Having experienced his kindness, I had come to him out of the blue, expecting an instant solution and now he had rejected me. "Perhaps it would help if I spoke to Lady Elspeth myself? I may be able to persuade her that Mr. Forres is not suitable for you?"

"No!" I was quite adamant on that point. I could imagine my aunt's reaction if a mere mechanic, however tall and handsome, arrived to speak on my behalf. "No, but I do thank you, Mr. Kemp. I shall endeavour to find another way out of my situation." I would return home. I would catch the next stage for the north and throw myself on my mother's mercy. Even if I had to live the remainder of my life as a spinster, I would not marry John Forres. But I wanted this man...

This very man who was speaking again. "All right. Give me a few days to find a solution, Miss Lamont. Come back a week today and I will see what I can do."

"A week! So long! I could be married before then." I expressed my dismay, but Mr. Kemp only shook that calm head.

"You will not be married before then. These affairs take time to arrange. There are guests to invite, a church to prepare, banns to be read, the minister to instruct, clothes and food to find..." he gave that slow smile I found so irritatingly fascinating. "No, Miss Lamont, I assure you that you will still be unwed this time next week."

"Oh, Mr. Kemp! I knew that you could help." Without thinking what I was doing, I rose, cupped his face in my hands and kissed him. Again he responded, but pulled away long before I was ready.

"Miss Lamont! You told me that you cannot marry John Forres because you loved another man. Think of him rather than thanking me so effusively!"

I looked at him in disbelief. Why did he not realise that he was the man I loved? Did I not make myself plain enough, or did Mr. Kemp believe that I kissed every mechanic that I came across? What kind of woman did he think I was?

"Yes, Mr. Kemp," I said. Remember I was only eighteen and very naïve. If only I had known that Willie Kemp was playing a double game and I was caught in the middle of a very elaborate trap, I would not have been so trusting. He was truly the most devious and wicked man alive!

Chapter Seven

That week was one of the longest that I have ever known. I put on my most demure face, obeyed every instruction that Aunt Elspeth chose to give, endured Louise's whining and constant mood changes and counted the hours.

"Oh Alison, are you not pleased to be marrying such a gentleman?" Aunt Elspeth would say, and I would simper and curtsey and think of his soft white hands.

"Yes, Aunt Elspeth."

"Oh Alison, please ensure that your hair is tidy today, for Mr. John Forres may call round."

"Oh yes, Aunt Elspeth," and I would scurry to the mirror and play with what loose strands of hair I had while Louise would watch and scowl and steal my hairbrush, the vicious little minx.

After a few days, Louise was less openly spiteful and began to take care of herself again, which a mixed blessing as the dressing tables once again resembled the battle of Maida with powder strewn everywhere and empty bottles scattered around like dead soldiers. I asked her if she had quite recovered from her disappointment.

"I have a man too," Louise told me, tossing that beautiful mane of blonde hair that sent her beaus wild with admiration and I always wanted to spoil with blue dye.

"Good," I said with my most false smile spread over my face. "I thought you would find someone. Who is it? That nice Mr. Semple?"

Semple was a near neighbour in George Street, a ruddy- faced man with broad shoulders and an amiable appearance.

"Oh no, it's not him. He has all the appearance of a farmer. Oh no, Alison, I have found somebody far more suitable. I have found a real gentleman with broad lands and a uniform."

"Ah," I said and wondered which of the unfortunate Highland officers had been fooled by Louise's charm. My countrymen are as brave as lions, but they are not always the best judge of female character. I think that they need a Highland woman to keep them right, or they can be up to any folly. "Who is this ideal man?"

"That's for me to know and you to wonder," Louise gave a little twirl so her dress rose around her perfect ankles. "So I'll leave you to your mirror, Alison. And do try and appear respectable, although I realise that it must be hard with hair like that."

"I'll do my best," I promised. "And shall I tell John that you have got over him?"

Her look could have cut glass. "Do what you will, Alison dear. You seem to do that anyway, without any permission from me. Or anybody else."

As you can imagine, that week passed abominably slowly. John Forres came to call twice, each time spending as much time in front of the mirror as he was in front of me, and the scent of his pomade lingered far longer than a memory of anything sensible he may have said.

"Is he not the perfect gentleman?" Aunt Elspeth asked. "What style he has. I envy you, Alison, being promised to such a man, although I really do not know why he prefers you to Louise."

About to say that they were welcome to each other, I thought it best to remain quiet. I did not want any hint of my possible plans to seep out. Mind you, I did not know what these plans were, but trusted entirely to the good judgement of Mr. Kemp: fool that I was "I am sure that I have no idea," I said, truthfully.

Pursing her lips as if she were preventing herself from making any comment, Aunt Elspeth swept away, her skirt an immaculate quarter inch from the floor and her back as erect as any scarlet- jacketed officer. I watched with admiration; in many ways, Lady Elspeth was the perfect woman and I could have learned a lot from her.

After a week of tormented worry, I again informed Aunt Elspeth that I required exercise to clear my thoughts.

She looked at me from above her imperious nose. "Clear your thoughts, Alison? I would imagine that you have thoughts only for Mr. John Forres."

"Oh I think of John Forres a lot," I said, "but there are other things in my mind as well. I must consider the guests, and the food, and the minister," I temporised desperately, trying to recall everything that Mr. Kemp had listed.

"Of course you must, but have we not been working on just these matters these last seven days?"

She had too, efficient old harridan that she was. Honestly, if they got rid of all these bumbling politicians and put Lady Elspeth and her ilk in charge of affairs, this country would run far better. It takes great skill and a lot of hard work to run a large household, my dears, and don't let anybody tell you different. What with the servants to manage, and the accounts, and ensuring that everything was up to what Lady Elspeth called *Edinburgh standards*, I had no idea how she found the time to arrange a wedding. But arranging it she was, and with utterly frustrating efficiency, so my days of freedom were fast slipping away frighteningly fast.

"Take Louise with you," Aunt Elspeth seemed to have a knack of simultaneously spoiling my plans and ruining my life. "The exercise will do her good. She has positively wilted since John Forres chose you over her."

I argued of course, but changing Aunt Elspeth's mind is as impossible as flying to the moon, so I was lumbered with my whining cousin as I promenaded along George Street. Despite her busy life, Aunt Elspeth took the time to escort us to the front door and stood there to bid us a good walk. She even watched us until we reached the corner of Hanover Street, which was most irritating but strangely touching. I nearly felt a pang of guilt as I waved my handkerchief in farewell, for although I was not sure how to lose Louise, I had no intention of returning to George Street for quite some time. At least until John Forres was happily engaged to some other suitable woman.

"Are the trees not pretty today?" I pointed to the stark branches of Queen Street Gardens, which Louise completely ignored. She had no time for anything of nature, except men.

"How far do you intend to walk?" she asked, already pretending to limp. "For my feet hurt. A lady should never walk, not when there are carriages and sedan chairs. It is far beneath our dignity."

"What is dignity on such a fine day as this?" I deliberately hurried down the steep slope that leads to Princes Street, hoping to tire Louise out or leave her trailing so far behind that she would not know what I was doing.

"Dignity is everything," Louise said. She clutched at my arm. "Oh *do* slow down Alison, you know how much I hate hurrying. It is so fatiguing."

I remembered her behaviour before we arrived at the Forres Residence on Hogmanay when she had left me to walk down that horrible wynd while she sat on comfort in the sedan chair. "Oh, Louise," I said. "Don't dawdle so. Let us be on and doing. After all, I have my John to think of, and you have your most mysterious beau." I teased her deliberately, but the results were not what I expected, as you will see by-and -by.

Rather than turning around and storming home, as I had hoped, Louise took hold of my arm and gripped so tightly that I feared she may bruise me. "I think you are perfectly horrid, Alison Lamont," she said, and she may well have been correct. "You know how much I admired John Forres, and you took him from me in front of everybody."

We had reached Princes Street now, where there were some splendid equipages slowly rolling past with the occupants admiring the view of the castle and the tumbled romance of the Old Town. Willie Kemp was not far away, sitting in his shed at the loch side, or tinkering with that foolish boat of his. I wished that I could get rid of Louise so I could run to him, for I had resolved to pour out all my feelings and chance his reaction. How could he refuse me? After all, I was a lady born and bred, and he was nothing, but very handsome with that enigmatic smile and that insufferable quiet confidence that was so unsuited to his station.

He was an infuriating man, Willie Kemp, as well as a devious blackguard but I did love him so. But at that moment, I did not know all that and I wanted nothing more than to see him and to lose the even more infuriating Louise Ballantyne.

"I have walked far enough," Louise announced, coming to a dead stop in the middle of the street and looking over toward the castle, where splashes of scarlet showed that sentinels were watching over us.

"You go back then," I said hopefully, "and I will continue. I have not nearly thought enough."

"Thought!" Louise's voice was scathing. "What is there to think about? You are just gloating because you stole my man from me!"

The suggestion was so absurd that I laughed openly, which was not the best idea in the world. I knew that Louise was unhappy, and I knew that she resented my engagement to John Forres, but until that minute she had been unable to really voice her disquiet. Even in the privacy of our shared bedroom, she could not tell me properly, in case some passing servant or even her mother was listening. But there were no servants here, and for once the street was clear of carriages.

"I hate you!" Louise's sudden scream frightened the seagulls that overwintered in the Nor' Loch so that a great flock exploded into frantic flight around our ears. "I hate you for taking John from me!"

I was so taken aback, for our family squabbles in Badenoch, although frequent, had not lasted so long or included so much vitriol as Louise could inject into only a few small words, I could only stare at her.

"You came to my house and immediately caused trouble!" Louise had dropped her voice to a sibilant hiss that was even more poisonous, and I felt my ears and cheeks burn. "I've spent my life looking for a man like John Forres and it's me he should marry, not you!" She was gripping both my arms and leaning close to me so her mouth was inches from my face and I could not escape her words.

"Louise," I said, and tried to sound stern. "Consider your position! You are behaving in a most unladylike fashion!"

Unfortunately, Louise was really too passionate to care about her position, and rather than withdraw, she took hold of my cloak and began to pull me this way and that. Now, as I have already indicated, I was not one of these nymph-like girls with no figure. I was a young lady of plentiful curves and the comfortable weight that naturally accompanies them, and I was really quite irritated at her behaviour, so I took hold of her and pushed back.

I realise, my dears, that you must be recoiling in horror at this disgraceful scene, but I feel that I must relate even the most shocking events in my young life, and wrestling with my cousin must rank high on that list. Louise was half a head taller than I, and two years older, but my centre of balance was lower so we were quite evenly matched, so within a few minutes we had crossed Princes Street, still struggling, and were tottering on the edge of the road. Now there were some people staring at us from their carriages, but we were too far gone in anger to take heed, and then one of us tripped, Louise screamed in my ear and we were both rolling hitherty-scitherty down the slope that led to the Nor' Loch.

Can you imagine the scene we must have provided? And can you imagine the scandal to my aunt? Two young, well brought up and respectable ladies rolling down a slope with our legs kicking, our skirts and petticoats flying and portions of bare ankle and even bare leg exposed for public view? My goodness, I am now an old and done lady I still feel ashamed, albeit slightly exhilarated, when I relive that event.

There were a few moments when the world seemed all topsy-turvy, with one minute Louise on top, and then me, but when we reached the muddy ground at the bottom we were still holding each other. Now, you would think that such an excitement would have dampened our ardour but not a bit of us. We hated each other heartily that day and no sooner had we risen than we were at it again, tongue lashing each other as we wrestled for supremacy.

It was Louise who wrenched her arm free first and swung a mighty slap that nearly took my head off. I screamed at the affront but retaliated with a slap of my own. I am still ashamed to admit, my dears, that there is little more satisfying in this world than landing an effective slap on somebody who richly deserves it. I can still feel the thrill of impact and see Louise stagger back, one hand to her face and her mouth working.

I followed, intent on satisfying myself further.

"You!" Louise screeched, much like a gutter-mouthed Newhaven fishwife, except without the propensity for hard work. "You..." she called me a few names that no lady should hear, yet alone know, and which I will refrain from writing down here. It's for your own good, my dears, so don't fret now. Perhaps your husbands will teach you these words if you annoy them suitably. Try driving his latest coach and scratching the bodywork: that should do the trick.

Of course, I retaliated in kind, for I have heard the servants talk and I was aware of the words, even if I was sometimes unsure of their meaning, so we were going at it hammer and tongs and no doubt terrifying any passing horses when Louise gave the choicest of insults.

"You are just a lion hunter," she said, inferring that I spent all my time chasing after men.

"I am not," I told her, "and you can keep your John Forres, and all the other Forreses. Indeed you can keep all the gentle born men in Edinburgh for I do not want them!"

"Oh no?" Louise sneered, standing back slightly and nearly staggering on the edge of the loch. She did not fall in, unfortunately. Perhaps I should have pushed her. "If you don't want them, who do you want? Some Highland chief perhaps? Do you expect some great poetical Ossian to come bounding out of the heather and carry you away?"

That slur on my Highland blood was too much. I finally lost all control, which is unusual for me. "Oh no," I told her. "I have a better man than any that are bred in the Highlands. I want Willie Kemp!"

As soon as the words were out of my mouth I regretted having said them, and the expression of mixed shock and triumph on Louse's face doubled my discomposure.

"You want Willie Kemp!" Her laugh was more painful than a dozen slaps, and I did not know what to do. I remember that I stood with my mouth open, staring at her, and then I begged, literally begged, her not to say anything.

"Oh, Alison! Oh, this is just priceless! Of course, I will tell people. I will tell everybody about the proud Highland princess who came to the capital in search of a husband!" She was mocking, with that great mane of hair floating around her perfect doll face and her lovely mouth as full as spite as anything I have ever seen.

"Please, Louise, please don't tell Aunt Elspeth!" I wondered if I should fall on my knees to plead. "Please don't."

"Oh, but I will," Louise stepped sideways, away from the loch. "I will tell everybody about your aspirations, my dear, darling cousin. I mean, you are hardly in the same class, are you?"

"I know," I admitted, more miserable than I had been for many years. "I am a gentlewoman and he is only a mechanic."

Louise stopped in mid- sentence and stared at me. "My, my," she said slowly and with exquisite relish. "You are indeed an ignorant little creature aren't you? You love him, don't you?"

I nodded. I seemed to be nodding a lot these past few days, while a variety of people interrogated me. That's the trouble with youth, dears, everybody thinks they have a right to know all your business. Well, take a tip from me and only tell somebody you can really trust, like your great-grandmother, and keep most to yourself.

"You really love Willie Kemp the mechanic; Willie Kemp!" She was laughing again, cutting cruelly at my fragmented pride. "Say it out loud and I might not tell anybody. Go on, shout it out."

I obeyed fool that I was, opening my mouth and shouting out the words that she fed me. "I love Willie Kemp!"

"Shout louder, cousin dear. Scream it with all your might or I will tell mother."

"I love Willie Kemp!" I yelled.

"Now shout that you love Willie Kemp even although he is only a mere artisan," her voice was pure poison.

"I love Willie Kemp, although he is only a mere artisan!" I yelled, hurting my throat with the effort.

"No," Louise shook her head so her blonde hair curled around her face. "I said 'even although' and you missed out the even." She stepped away, heading for the banking that led to Princes Street. "So I will tell mama right away, and then you will really be in trouble." She paused, one leg stretched before her as she spoke over her shoulder. "You've never seen mama in a real stinking temper. Oh, Alison, I would not like to be you when you get back, but I'm already looking forward to it!" Quite forgetting her sore feet, she scrambled up that bank, squared her shoulders and hurried off with her tale.

I watched her go, quite deflated and with my eyes prickling, but worse was to come. I do not know how long I stood there; it might have been ten seconds or two minutes but to me, it seemed like a lifetime. If I had known what was to come I might have stepped into the loch and bid a sad farewell to the world, but we cannot tell the future, you see. In the days to come, I was to say "good day" to my husband and "adieu" to Willie Kemp, but fate had to use me ill first, as you will see.

"So, Miss Lamont." The voice was familiar but unwelcome at that time as I turned around to see Willie Kemp staring at me. "What was all that noise about?"

I shook my head. "It doesn't matter," I said, but already the tears were streaking my cheeks.

"Come and talk to me," he invited, and his hand was comforting around my shoulder as he escorted me around the loch. Only when I was back inside that familiar shed and sitting by the same old fire with a mug of hot soup in my hand, did he crouch at my side.

"I heard what was said," Mr. Kemp told me, and my tears began in earnest.

"I'm sorry," I said, "but I did not know how to tell you."

"Ah," Mr. Kemp said, as calm and in control as ever. "So when you told me about this man that you love, that was me?"

"Yes," I said and looked at him in hope of a reciprocal announcement. Instead, Mr. Kemp shook his head sensibly.

"But would it work out, Miss Lamont? I am very flattered of course, a good looking, no, a very good looking gentlewoman like you and me, a mere artisan?"

For a moment I thought that he was laughing at me, but then his eyes returned to their normal solemn brown. "But you do like me," I reminded him. "We have kissed…"

"We have," he admitted. "And very pleasant it was too. But I believe that you have also exchanged kisses with Mr. John Forres?"

"Only one kiss," I denied that I would do such a thing more than once. "And it was not a very pleasant one."

"Apparently Mr. Forres does not agree if he wants to marry you."

"You kissed me more than once," I pointed out, with my voice a trifle tart.

"I am fully aware of that, but even a score of kisses is not a sound basis for a successful marriage," Mr. Kemp said, quietly. "And that is especially true for a marriage where the two participants are from such different backgrounds."

"I cannot go back now," I said, suddenly sober, "Louise will tell Aunt Elspeth what I said." I looked up as another thought struck me. "She will also inform John Forres."

"Surely that is no bad thing," Mr. Kemp remained crouched at my side. I saw the streak of black oil on his forearms and wondered if I could spend the rest of my life with an artisan who tinkered with machines. Strangely, the idea did not concern me in the slightest. "If Mr. John Forres hears about your attraction to a mechanic, he might break off the engagement."

"No," I shook my head once more. Really, I am surprised that my head was still attached to my neck, the number of times it was shaken back then. "They will lock me in my room to ensure that I am at the wedding. John Forres has announced that he will marry me, and what

I have seen of the man assures me that he is too proud to go back on his word."

"I understand." Mr. Kemp stood up in a single swift movement. "Only one thing remains to be done, then."

"And what is that, pray?" I waited for Mr. Kemp's pronouncement, fully expecting that he would take me back to my aunt. I had quite forgotten our earlier agreement. That is the consequence of arguing, you see, it drives away all sensible thoughts from your head. It is always best to keep clear thoughts, my dears, and avoid hot blood.

"I must take you somewhere safe, as we already decided." His smile was as gentle as any doting father, and I would have loved to throw myself into his arms, despite the smears of oil. Instead, I merely ducked my head.

"Thank you, Mr. Kemp," I said, and I really meant it.

When I look back on that day, I should remember that decision of Mr. Kemp's, and the total change it made in my life, but I do not. Instead I remember that resounding slap that I landed on Louse's pretty face. Indeed, I must admit that it is one of my most treasured memories. I only wish that I had been able to land another.

Chapter Eight

I had expected that Mr. Kemp would have to make a number of arrangements for our journey to God knew where, but instead, he insisted that we leave virtually immediately.

"But Mr. Kemp," I protested, for I was unused to such hurried departures. "Why the rush?"

"Because, my dear, the second that your beloved cousin informs Lady Elspeth what you said, I suspect Her Ladyship will race here hot-foot."

I nodded. Aunt Elspeth could indeed be an impetuous woman when she was not being infuriatingly efficient. I looked to the door, half expecting her to burst it open and thrust inside, brandishing her parasol and a certificate of marriage. "My goodness, Mr. Kemp, let us be off indeed."

It was only when we had travelled a good quarter mile from the loch, in a direction opposite to Edinburgh, that I thought to enquire where we were going.

"To a little place I know where you will be very snug and quite secure," Mr. Kemp told me, unsmiling. "And it is a place that I doubt that Mr. John Forres would ever venture, although I am not so sure about your aunt." He smiled at me again. "Lady Elspeth is quite a formidable woman."

We walked as far as the Village of Dean, by the Water of Leith, and here Mr. Kemp hired a small horse for me. I did not hear the details of the transaction, for he asked me to wait in the lee of one of the mills, whose wheel churned the water white in a manner reminiscent of the steam boat on the Nor' Loch.

"You mount up," Mr. Kemp ordered gently, "and I will lead. Did you bring a cloak?"

I had only my light pelisse; it was pretty, with fine stitching, but was more suited for the dictates of town fashion than the rigours of the Scottish winter. Mr. Kemp, that forward- thinking man, had found a heavy travelling cloak in bottle green, which he slipped around my shoulders. Strangely, it was scented with some perfume that was slightly familiar, but I could not say where I had experienced it before.

With Mr. Kemp walking at my side, we walked up-river. So far that January we had been lucky, but now the rain started, weeping through the network of branches above and dripping down upon us. I huddled into my new cloak but poor Mr. Kemp had only his jacket to cover him. He did not complain but walked solidly onward as we passed the various small villages and chuntering mills that lined the Water of Leith.

Now I will not bore you with the tedium of travel, but suffice to say that it is around fourteen miles from the Village of Dean to Malleny Mills on the outskirts of the Pentland Hills, and by the time we arrived I was drooping in the saddle. I am a reasonable rider, but parts of me were distinctly uncomfortable after the haul on the rough road, and I am sure that Mr. Kemp was also fatigued, although he did not show it.

We had spoken of many things during that walk, and I had got to know Mr. Kemp a little better. I now knew more about engineering than I cared, but I also knew more about the fish and wildlife of the river, the name of just about every person we met on the road and even the politics of the French Wars. Of anything that mattered, and in particular of Mr. Kemp's feelings for me, not a whiff did I have.

I knew then that Mr. Kemp would be a good man to trust with a secret, for he told only what he wanted you to know.

"We will stay here the night," he said quietly, "if you would care to dismount?"

I obeyed at once and tried to ease the stiffness from my nether quarters without being seen, for of course, a lady must never admit to even possessing such parts when in the company of a gentleman, or even Willie Kemp. If he noticed my discomfort, he did not say. "Where are we?" I asked for we had stopped at a rather imposing tower a mile or so past the mills and at the head of a short but breathless rise.

"Bavelaw," he told me. "Now you wait here while I find us somewhere to sleep, and something to eat."

"Be careful, Mr. Kemp," I warned, and for the first time I realised that my behaviour could well get him into trouble. I told him so, and he gave that slow smile that I was getting used to.

"Thank you for the thought," he said, seriously, "but don't you worry about me. I'm quite well known around here. After all, mechanics and artisans are rather a rare commodity." He smiled again, patted the pony and stalked toward the tower house.

I say stalked with meaning, for he had a long loping stride that was very familiar to me. I had seen the like many times on the hill men of Badenoch, and suddenly I realised from where my attraction for Mr. Kemp came. Perhaps, I thought, it was not Willie Kemp with whom I was in love, but the familiarity that he portrayed?

I shook my head. No, that could not be. I could not have made that mistake.

It was nearly fifteen minutes before Mr. Kemp returned and he was smiling. "It is all serene, my dear. It is arranged that we will sleep in the kitchen tonight, and the horse will be stabled and fed."

I chose to ignore the familiarity of that *my dear* and instead voiced my concern about the arrangements he had made. "In the kitchen?" I am not sure what I expected, but I had known only the best all my life. Although I knew that Willie Kemp was of a lower social standing, I was not prepared for everything that gulf in class would entail. After all, kitchens were for servants and I was a gentlewoman.

"Yes, we'll be nice and warm there and safe from questions. I know these people and nothing will reach Lady Elspeth's ears that she does not already know, and that is a promise."

The servants seemed quite amused to greet us, treating Mr. Kemp with far more respect than the rough humour they used on me, but they were pleasant enough and made us welcome in their own way. To be honest, my dears, I found them easier company than many of their so- called betters, and they provided us with a warm place to sleep for the night. I shared a tiny cupboard; I really cannot call it a room, with a couple of bright young Abigails. They retired a little before midnight and were up well before dawn but between times they slept like corpses. I was not sure where Mr. Kemp spent the night hours and I confess I barely gave the matter much thought, but he seemed very refreshed in the morning.

"Are you sure that nobody will tell the master?" I did not know who owned this Bonaly Tower, but the owner would certainly know Aunt Elspeth.

Mr. Kemp just gave that infuriatingly slow smile. "You have nothing to worry about, Miss Lamont. As I have already explained, your aunt will not hear anything that she does not already know." He leant closer. "I know these people. You can trust them."

I liked Bonaly Tower. It was an old place of solid grey walls set within wooded policies, washed by the winter rain and soft with the breath of the Pentland Hills. I liked it better than anywhere I had been since I came south, and it lifted my spirits when I again sat on the pony's side-saddle and headed for the heights.

Now, you girls should know this part of the world, but in case you have forgotten, I will give you a quick reminder. The Pentlands are a range of low hills that begin a few miles south of Edinburgh and stretch about twenty miles south -west. The hills in the north are close together and relatively steep, while in the south they are broader and lonelier. Although only a few people live within the heather slopes, there are weaving and agricultural settlements around the fringes, while shepherds and cattle drovers actually traverse the heights and slaps, as we call the passes.

Mr. Kemp seemed as happy striding through the Pentland Hills as he had sitting in his boat in the Nor' Loch. I watched him from the corner of my eye, and fell in love all over again. While in his shed he had been an artisan and a hard working mechanic on the steam boat, here he was a man of the hills, perfectly at home in the heather.

"You have been here before, Mr. Kemp," I accused, and he grinned to me. Not just his usual careful smile, but a full- blooded grin.

"Once or twice," he admitted.

"I thought that you lived by the loch," I was beginning to think that Willie Kemp was not everything he seemed to be.

"I do, sometimes." Mr. Kemp was back to his usual enigmatic self as he lifted his head and, if anything; increased the length of his stride.

I liked the Pentland Hills on first sight. I liked the shapes and the small, intimate scale compared to my native Badenoch, I liked the sough of the wind in the heather and the friendly bubbling burns, but most of all I liked the people. Hill people are probably the same every-where, self- reliant, slightly wilder than those on the level ground but sound as a church bell at bottom.

"Where are you taking me?"

"I am taking you somewhere that Lady Elspeth will not come," Mr. Kemp told me. The further we travelled, the more relaxed he be-came.

I sighed and again tried to draw a commitment from him. "You know that I love you," I told him.

"I know that you have told me so," Mr. Kemp said. He continued to walk, stepping across a small burn without breaking stride. "This is the Kitchen Moss," he spread his hand as if he were granting me a favour.

I looked across a heather moor, gloomy but not unfriendly under the drizzling rain. "I told you it because it's true," I said, realising that he had avoided revealing any feelings at all.

Mr. Kemp did not reply to that, but led me into the heart of the moor, skirting the occasional peat hole with so much familiarity that he must have known these hills as well as he knew his own hut.

"Where are you taking me, Mr. Kemp?"

"You will see," was all he said, and within fifteen minutes we were ascending a great lump of a hill, with a straggle of Scots Pine trees leading us to the summit and a view of half Scotland stretching before us.

"This is Harper's Hill," Mr. Kemp told me, "although people are beginning to change the name to Cairn Hill because of the cairn of stones on top." He indicated a distant mound, scarcely visible in the drifting mist and rain.

"I like Harper's Hill better," I told him. "It's more romantic."

"It certainly is," Mr. Kemp approved my choice. "It was said that the ancient druids used to play their harps here, hence the name."

I nodded, imagining the druids in their long white coats living on these hills. Hills without stories are only pretty: hills with stories have a character all of their own. Badenoch had been full of legends and stories, from the days of Ossian and the times of the clans to tales of Bonnie Prince Charlie and Cluny Macpherson. It was good to know that these gentler hills also had their share of the old legends. Somewhere above us, the call of a hunting bird accentuated the loneliness, and then, when we had walked for some time, I saw the future Mr. Kemp had planned for me.

It was a small cottage sitting deep in a hope, a tiny closed valley. Above and all around was the heather moor, and there was not even the smoke of a human habitation for miles.

"You want me to live there?"

I was shocked. I was a gentlewoman born and bred, used to servants and soft living. Possibly more importantly, I was not used to being alone. In Badenoch, there was always my brothers and sisters and as many servants as anybody would need. Even in Edinburgh, I had Louise in the same room and my aunt and her household within call. Here, deep in the swell of the Pentlands, I had nobody, except maybe Willie Kemp.

And the cottage was tiny. Hardly larger than Mr. Kemp's hut, it had drystone unmortared walls two rooms and a stone necessary built outside the walls. The roof was of heather thatch that matched the surroundings so perfectly that it was hard to see where the building ended and the hillside began. I fought the prickle of tears that threatened to embarrass me in front of Mr. Kemp.

"Do you like it?" Mr. Kemp seemed vastly pleased with himself. "You wanted me to find you somewhere that neither your aunt nor John Forres would find; I believe I have done exactly that."

"You have indeed," I agreed, somewhat reluctantly. My aunt would never venture to such an out of the way place, and John Forres would hardly put a delicate foot out of doors yet alone venture into these wild hills.

Mr. Kemp smiled. "Come inside." I was glad to see that, despite the remoteness, there was a key for the front door, and that the inside was clean if Spartan in its lack of amenities.

The front room had a plain deal table and two chairs, with a small black fireplace complete with a pail of coal and a pile of kindling.

"There's peat stacked outside," Mr. Kemp told me helpfully. "You do know how to start a fire, don't you?"

I nodded, glad of my childhood in Badenoch when we had roamed the Monadhliath mountains at will; lifting trout from the burn had always necessitated a small fire for cooking.

"There is some food hanging in the larder," Mr. Kemp showed me a tiny cupboard with hooks from which joints of meat and lumps of fish hung. There were also baskets of vegetables and apples. "So you won't starve."

"And there are books."

There were two shelves of them, showing a catholic taste. I noticed Voltaire and Burns, the latest Walter Scott and a few Gothic romances side-by-side with classic tales of Swift and poems of Ferguson as well as heavier tomes of philosophy and science, geography and religion. There was even one in Gaelic, which I lifted like an old friend.

The second room boasted a wide bed with a rustling straw mattress and a bedside table with an oval mirror and a vase of winter roses.

"You put these there," I accused, hopefully.

"I did not," Mr. Kemp denied. "Well, my dear; what do you think of your new home?"

I was not sure. Although it was exactly what I had wanted, I was afraid. Life is like that, my dears, we constantly bang on the door to get inside our dreams, and the minute we are in, we want out. We never appreciate what, or who, we have. For one fleeting instant, I knew that John Forres would never have expected his wife to live in such a place. And then I looked at Willie Kemp and wondered what he was thinking.

He was wearing an expression that I had never seen before, and I realised that he was anxious. He really wanted me to like this cottage that he had found, and I suspected, furnished, for me, and I knew that I could not hurt him.

"It's beautiful," I said, and only I knew that I lied. Honestly, I felt like crying, to think that I had given up all the comfort of Edinburgh's New Town, and all the definite luxury of the Forres lands and estate, for a hovel, and for Willie Kemp. And I he had still never made any commitment to me, besides those few fleeting kisses.

"Good," he nodded, and his expression changed.

"It's like our own little love nest," I said and immediately regretted the words as I suddenly realised where I was.

I was alone in a very out of the way place with a man who was a virtual stranger. Nobody knew that we were here, and nobody could trace me. Bred by years of gothic romances, the horrible thought came to me that Willie Kemp might have lured me here for purposes other than love. Perhaps he only wanted to slake his lust – and that phrase was also from the gothic romances. The brutal reality was of cruelty and sordid humiliation. What better place could there be than a lonely cottage deep in the moors?

I looked at him with horror, and I am sure that I whimpered, but Mr. Kemp made no lustful advances as they did in all the worst books, he did not extend his evil arms, nor did he growl menacingly or leer at me from narrowed eyes. Indeed he only smiled, as if secretly amused.

"Good. Now I am afraid that I must leave you, Miss Lamont."

The words struck me like a blow. "Leave me? Are we not to live together here?"

"I must work on my boat," Mr. Kemp, that evil, wicked, deceitful man said, putting his mechanical tinkering before me, the hopeful love of his life.

"But Mr. Kemp…" I looked around at the suddenly bleak and chilling hills, with their terrible stories of druids and no doubt of human sacrifice. "I have never been alone before."

"I am afraid it cannot be helped," he said, unfeelingly. "I know some of the local shepherds. I will ensure that they pop in every few days to ensure that you are safe."

"Shepherds?" I am sure my voice must have betrayed my panic and disdain. In Badenoch, you see, we did not have a high opinion of sheep and shepherds. The great evictions had already started; what you may know as the Highland Clearances, when the Highland glens were cleared of the tenancy, which made little money, to make way for sheep, which were profitable. Indeed we had a rhyme in Gaelic that gave our feelings for these wooly monsters.

Mo bheannachd aig na balgairean
A chionn bhi sealg nan caorach.

The words translate as

"*My blessings on the foxes*
Because they kill the sheep."

"Our Pentland shepherds are a decent bunch," Mr. Kemp assured me when I related my feelings. "You need have no fear of them."

I think I may have stared stupidly at him as the realisation was driven further home. I would now be living as a recluse, a virtual hermit in this tiny cottage, with nothing to look forward to but a possible visit by a shepherd. Had I really swapped my comfortable life for this? Suddenly marriage to John Forres did not seem so bad. True, he was an obnoxious man, but I would only be with him for a few hours each day, if that, and I would be mistress of huge estates, able to come and go as I pleased, with a bevy of admirers and friends.

I fought off the tears. You see, my dears, sometimes life is not as you expect, but one must just accept it and strive for better times. I had chosen this life of my own free will, and, as the old saying tells us, *she that tholes overcomes*. It was my time of enduring, I had made my bed and I must lie in it … Och, you can add any other proverb you can think of.

Oh God, girls, don't believe all these old wives tales! Take it from me, an old wife, that there is always a choice and sitting *waiting* for a better time is not the answer. Fight for yourselves, girls. Take the world by the throat and shake every advantage out of it, make sure you have a comfortable, happy life and forget all this nonsense about patient enduring. Life is too short to suffer through.

"One last thing," said my smiling tormentor. "This cottage is on Cairnsmuir land, so be careful not to wander too close to Cairnsmuir House."

"Cairnsmuir? Mrs. Cairnsmuir?" I well-remembered that evil old harridan who had asked the most penetrating questions.

"That's the very lady," Mr. Kemp said, "I'd better return the pony to its proper owner." And he slipped away without even a goodbye or a parting kiss.

I must confess that I sat down and cried. Although I had got exactly what I wanted, and there are those who may say I got exactly what I deserved, and they may be right, I was not a happy lassie. Here I was, a gentlewoman, stuck in a tiny cottage in the middle of nowhere, cut off from everything I had once known and for what? In return, I had the memory of a few kisses and the feeling that I might love Mr. Willie Kemp the artisan.

The more I contemplated my position, the more foolish I felt, but once I had committed myself, what was the alternative? Could I return home with my tail between my legs and hope for a welcome like the prodigal niece? Hardly. After all, after spending a night with a man, my reputation would be in shreds: it was not likely that John Forres would want anything to do with me, nor, for that matter, would any respectable man, yet alone a gentleman with lands.

I had, in truth, ruined my life, and it was nobody's fault but my own.

I must have cried half that day, but when the well of tears finally ran dry, I realised that I had not bettered my position in the slightest. So I picked myself up, checked what there was to eat and cut myself a slice of bread and cheese. Good bread too and the cheese had a fine, nutty tang. The knife, I noted, had the same crown and crossed sword motif as there had been on Mr. Kemp's brushes in the shed, and I resolved to ask him from where they came if he ever came back for me.

But what if he did not?

That thought terrified me, so I pushed it away and decided to explore my surroundings.

Luckily the rain had stopped so it was easy to walk up the heathery slope immediately behind my cottage and look at the hills. January is always a bitterly cold month in Scotland, so I was glad of Mr. Kemp's heavy travelling cloak as I tramped up the dead heather, holding my skirt with my left hand and swinging my right for better balance. Now, you will know that walking in the hills can be exhilarating, or fun, or downright exhausting, but sometimes the wilds can be a dismal place. It all depends on your mood.

When I had travelled with Kemp, the Pentlands had been a magical place, full of promise and fun, with shapely hills and the smooth burr of hidden burns, but once I was alone, the whole atmosphere altered. They immediately assumed a sombre outlook, dark and grim, with the grey skies oppressive and the deep silences accusing me of abandoning my true life.

I did not enjoy that afternoon as I viewed the grey-green slopes and listened to the constant rustle of that unforgiving wind that seemed to be plucking at me as if determined to remove me from the slope and deposit me back down in the low country. I felt unwanted there, an intruder into a place that I did not belong, and I soon scurried back to the cottage. There was a tinder box for the fire and enough fuel for the night, so I did not freeze, but I was certainly not warm and cosy. I also had no maid to keep the flames alive, and nobody with whom to argue or discuss the world.

I did read, but books are no consolation for company. I could not concentrate on words that danced across the page with my wayward thoughts, and I truly contemplated leaving that place and walking back to Edinburgh. One look outside persuaded me to stay, however, for the weather had closed in with the night and sleeting rain hammered at the stone walls and clamoured at the small windows. I was all alone in a tiny cottage, trapped by weather and circumstances and feeling very sorry for myself.

With nothing better to do, I had a brief wash and went to bed. But not to sleep, for all I could hear was the howl of the wind around the eaves and the batter of rain on the tiny window. I lay there for much of the night, full of self- pity as I wept. I, who had so recently despised Louise for her tears, cried away that night.

Morning brought only gloom as the unrelenting hills showed me no pity. The rain continued, and the fire had gone out. I had forgotten how much labour was involved in raking the grate and rebuilding with paper and kindling, with hands red with cold and a stomach hollow with hunger, for I was too cold to eat.

Suffice to say, my dears, that I was unhappy in that darling little cottage, and I remained that way for some two days. Solitary days mark you, for my oh-so-handsome Willie Kemp did not come to visit and I was left with only his memory and those already fading winter roses.

What can I tell you of that time alone in that stark cottage? Not a great deal, for one day was like the dismal next and all the time I waited, hoping for the door to open and Mr. Kemp to walk in. Love is like that, you see, all the hardships and confusion of the early relationships matter less than a tear in the Atlantic Ocean once your sweetheart smiles to you. All you live for is the sound of his voice, or the sight of his face, or one whiff of the tobacco he stuffs in his pipe and when you have that, all your troubles are small and your day has been worthwhile.

Well, I waited for any of these things, and not a damned one came. Pardon my language dears, but even now I can recall the long drear days when I had to fend for myself and I thought that Willie Kemp, like love and hope, had deserted me. By the third day, I knew my surroundings so well, despite the rain, that I wandered further than my wont, and I saw a sight that brought home to me exactly how bitter was my plight.

There was enough food in the cottage to last me the winter, and enough fuel outside to keep Edinburgh warm, yet alone one small building, so there was nothing to keep me occupied save reading. I knew the best of the books by heart and had little interest in anything intellectual, so I was soon bored. Throwing on that heavy cloak of Mr. Kemp's, I took to walking. At first, I kept close to the cottage, but that soon palled, so I ventured further.

On my second and longer walk, I started when I saw a shadowy figure vanish below the skyline of heather, and I wished I had brought a stick. I gave a long halloo to prove I was not scared but succeeded only in hurting my throat. When I ascended the ridge, there was nobody to be seen, so I shrugged off the feeling that I was being watched. It was probably the local shepherd, I told myself, for the Pentlands were infested with sheep. You could hardly move for tripping over the things with their great wooly bodies and their jaws always munch-munch-munching twenty to the dozen.

Anyway, I walked further than I intended, and was I came to a great house. I had thought that these hills were as desolate as the Monadhliath, so the sight of a civilised abode placed in the middle of the waste was very surprising. As you know, I was brought up in large houses, and I could recognise a good house from a poor one, and the property I saw that day would have passed muster among top quality buildings anywhere in the world. Oh, it was not the largest I have seen, far from it or even the grandest, but it screamed elegance from every stone and slate that had built it. The designer, or architect, whoever he was, knew his job and had created a building that merged perfectly with the hills, yet retained so much dignity and style that I nearly curtsied as soon as I crested the hill and looked upon it.

I did not know the name, but crept closer, attracted by the beauty especially when compared to my own poor condition. I soon wished that I had remained at a distance, for the ground floor windows were open and the sound of laughter and gaiety came forth. Shivering in the persistent Pentland drizzle, I huddled behind a tree, for the policies were well wooded and immaculately groomed, and looked inside.

They were dancing. I hated the idea of people dancing and living a normal life while I suffered in a peasant's shack. And then I recognised them; there was Mrs. Cairnsmuir, laughing with Alexander Forres, there was a group of officers, resplendent in their kilts and scarlet, and there was my beloved cousin, Louise. I stared at her for a long moment. Did she not care that I was missing? Why was she not out scouring the streets of Edinburgh or these benighted hills?

Feeling completely wretched, I watched as Louise took hold of a man and led him from that chandelier-lit dance hall. A light flickered and flared and I saw them appear at a window upstairs, laughing together and obviously happy in each other's company. I recognised the man as one of the French prisoners of war from Lady Catriona's ball, and I swallowed away my misery. When even French prisoners were having a better time than me, I knew that there was something seriously amiss with the world. At that moment I truly hated my life, myself and especially Willie Kemp, damn his scheming hide. I did not know then, that I would soon meet my husband.

Chapter Nine

The snow came on the seventh day, and the cold cottage became positively Baltic, with ice forming on the inside of the window and my breath coming in clouds. I forced myself to leave its meagre shelter to drag in peat from the stack outside, and I looked anew at these once-friendly Pentland Hills.

Now they were stark and drear and bitter. Snow has the ability to harden the edges of hills and increase their apparent height, so I was a dwarf in a landscape fashioned by winter giants. Even with Mr. Kemp's cloak on, I was cold, but there was no peat left in the house and I had to gather fuel from the outside stack. That meant using a spade to break the surface frost and taking the blocks, piece by piece inside the house. That was a hard job, my dears, so don't let anybody tell you that country life was idyllic in the old days. It was hard work, pure and simple, and to be lax was to freeze or starve. I thought I might do both that morning when I realised that there was no water left.

If I had been sensible, I would have melted some of the abundant snow, but instead, I took the pail and walked down to the burn, slithering and falling with nearly every step. Women's boots, you know, are not designed for hard usage. Men's boots, however, are and I felt a new kind of chill when I saw the unmistakable imprint of a man's foot in the snow. It was a large footprint, and two of the nails in the heel, I remember, were slightly askew.

I had thought myself safe in this remote cottage, and then I recalled that shadowy shape I had seen the day I saw Louise with that Frenchman. I was obviously not alone out here, and how desperately I wished that Willie Kemp would appear to take me somewhere less dangerous, where I had some company and there were no strange men haunting the heights.

"Oh Mr. Kemp," I breathed. "Please come soon!"

The burn was beyond freezing, so cold that I could barely put my hand in it, but needs must so I broke the surface ice, dipped in the pail and scooped up enough water for my needs. As you can imagine, I was not happy, but as my tears only froze on my cheeks I soon stopped crying, save for the odd sniff or two, and carried on.

It is hard to describe my feelings at that time. Did I regret leaving Aunt Elspeth's house? Well, yes. Very much and I was very tempted to go back, but my stubborn pride bade me remain. Did I regret running from a marriage to John Forres? Yes, when I considered that the alternative was a lifetime of suffering and toil; marriage is only part of your life, my dears, and very few marriages are conducted on the basis of equality and constant romance. Some are, mind, and if you can find a man that will give you that, then dig your nails in deep and hang on for grim death.

However, at that minute, with my feet wet and cold, my breath clouding uncomfortably around my face and a bucket of freezing water slopping around my legs, romance was the last thing on my mind. Whatever the future held, living like some mediaeval peasant was not my ideal choice, and I resolved to escape from this life of drudgery as quickly as I could. I had been in this rural idyll for a week, you see, and that was more than enough for me.

Stamping my feet to keep them warm, I headed back to the cottage. I had perhaps a hundred yards to walk, all uphill, and carrying a full pail of water. Of course I slipped, and of course I fell, and of course, the contents of that pail cascaded over me.

Now, ordinarily, such a scene would be funny, as long as it happened to somebody else, but when you are living out in the wild, and you have to create your own heat, such an event is serious. I lay on the ground for just an instant before rising and hurrying as quickly as I could back to the cottage.

By the time I reached the front door, my fingers and toes were numb, and most other parts were not far behind, so I piled peat and wood on the still smouldering fire with no thought about saving some for the evening, and began to strip off my clothes. I knew that I had to get warm as quickly as I could, or pneumonia might set in, so I wasted no time, peeling off everything and leaving them strewn around the room. Normally a maid would be there to tidy up after me, but not this time. You have no idea how we depend on servants until they are not there.

I am here to tell you my dears, that there is no fire quite as warming as a peat fire flame. It is gentle and kindly, yet gives a heat that seeps into your bones. Coal is somehow harsher, and poor quality coal can split and spark, which is not advisable when you are crouching a foot away from the flames in the same state of innocence as Eve.

Strangely, I was quite enjoying the warmth when the door opened and Mr. Kemp walked in. He later claimed that he had knocked, but I was never sure whether to believe him or not, but my initial reaction was to cover myself. I immediately realised the irony, that he should catch me in the same state of undress, and for a similar reason, that I had caught him, and then I also remembered my thoughts on that occasion.

After my initial embarrassment, I had enjoyed the novel view, and indeed that incident remains one of my fondest memories, something that I unlock from its cabinet on the cold winter's nights. After all, I am an old lady now, so must be allowed to indulge in my fantasies. Do not allow pointless guilt to ruin your life, my dears; we all share the same feelings, to a greater or lesser degree, and despite what propriety would force upon us, I think it is natural to savour the attractions of the opposite sex: if it were not, then there would be no babies born and where would that leave us all?

I saw the same shock displayed on Mr. Kemp's face as I remember feeling myself, but rather than cringe away, I stood proud. After all, if I had pleasurable memories, then surely he must also be allowed the same. My but I was a proud hussie, was I not? Holding his eyes, I dropped my hands to my side.

"Mr. Kemp," I said, as formally as if we were in Aunt Elspeth's withdrawing room. I dropped in a curtsey, aware that his eyes had strayed from mine for more than a fraction of a second.

He turned around quickly, covering his face. "A thousand apologies," he said, and it was the first, and I believe the only, time that I heard him stutter.

"Mr. Kemp," I said, in charge of the situation for once. "There is no need to apologise. But please close the door."

Rather than have him escape into the cold, I forestalled him by walking past, naked as I was, and pushing the door to.

"Mr. Kemp," I said again. "Do you not like what you see?"

Now my dears, you may think me bold to the point of wanton, a shameless hussy and anything but a gentlewoman, but my generation lived by different rules. This present queen and her German husband, Albert something-or-other-that-I-cannot-pronounce, have changed the nature of society. We had none of your stuffiness. We believed that life was for living, and we played fast and loose with chance. Gambling was a passion, and we could gamble with our emotions and lives as easily as with cards dice and money.

Still with his back turned, Mr. Kemp said nothing.

"Did you not hear me, Mr. Kemp?" I took the two steps toward him, put my hand on his shoulder and spun him around. Now, that should have been an impossible task, for he was a tall man and as strong as any blacksmith born, but it seemed that the simple pressure from my forefinger was enough. He turned toward me, still with one hand covering his eyes.

"Mr. Kemp," I said, and I could hear a strange huskiness in my voice that I had never heard before. "Am I to accept the fact that you find the sight of me offensive?"

"Indeed no," he said, "Quite the reverse, but it is not right that I should look..."

"In what way is it not right?" I asked, but then I knew that Mr. Kemp was a gentleman in the true and proper sense of the word. He had walked in on me when I was at my most vulnerable, and he took no advantage.

"My dear Miss Lamont," he said, and I swear there was a tremor in his voice. "Pray cover yourself."

I stepped back, rustled the dry clothes that I had placed on the table, and said. "There you are."

When he uncovered his eyes I was as naked as before.

"Miss Lamont!"

But this time I was too quick for him and held his hands before he could raise them to his face. Again it was strange how a weak woman like me could control such a powerful man.

He looked at me frankly as I watched his eyes, and only when I was ready did I turn, and walk slowly to my dry clothes. His hands were still by his side when he reached the table, but he was not smiling. There was nothing to frighten a girl in that solemn, thoughtful face.

"Indeed I do like what I see," he told me frankly. "And there is nothing offensive to my eyes."

"Then we are equally matched," I was still in command of the situation. "For I liked what I saw in your shed by the loch."

I had expected him to colour up, as he had done before, but instead he gave that slow smile. "You are the only woman to have ever seen me like that save my mother."

"Ah," I smiled back as I began to dress. I had no fear, you see, that he would attempt to ravish me, and no embarrassment at all in front of Willie Kemp. You should never have fear or embarrassment with the man you love, my dears, and if you have either, then I ask you to examine your love thoroughly, for something is not right. "Unfortunately, I cannot say the same. You are not the first of your sex to see me as nature intended."

"No?" His head came up at once, as I had hoped it would, but he was too much of a gentleman to enquire further.

I allowed the thought to torment him a little longer as I completed hauling on my underthings and moved on to the next layer of clothing. "I have three brothers," I said and enjoyed the sudden relaxation of his face. I completed his education with a smile, a twist of my hips that I learned from Louise and a few significant words. "But they are the only ones to have seen me *au naturalle*, and not for many years."

There was warm light behind his eyes now, and I needed only say one more thing to capture him completely, I thought.

"I do not intend any other man save you to see me in a state of undress."

Was that not as good as a marriage proposal? Was I not hinting as hard as I could that I wanted to marry him, despite our difference in social standing?

"Many men would be sorry to hear you say that," Willie Kemp made a gallant attempt at a compliment, but again sidestepped the main question. Would that man never commit himself to me?

I completed my dressing with my first feeling of humiliation that day. "I am glad that you have finally arrived Mr. Kemp." It was difficult to regain my dignity only seconds after offering him everything that I had, but I tried my best. "For there is a strange man lurking around this cottage."

"Is there?" Mr. Kemp raised his eyebrows. He seemed more comfortable speaking with a fully dressed woman. "What sort of strange man, Miss Lamont, and when did you see him?"

"I have not seen him," I admitted, "but I thought I saw someone in the hills a few days ago, and there was a footprint in the snow."

"You saw a footprint in the snow!" Mr. Kemp shook his head. I swear he was mocking me. "And was this footprint also lurking around the cottage?"

It was obvious that Mr. Kemp was not taking my position seriously.

"It could have been anyone," I said, quite desperate to make him understand the danger I could have been in. "A murderer, even a Frenchman!"

Mr. Kemp gave his slow smile. "It was neither," he said. "Believe me, I would hear about any strangers lurking about your cottage."

Strangely, as soon as he said those words, I knew that it was true. For a mechanic, Mr. Kemp had a presence that I could not fathom. He could certainly put on as many airs and graces as an English factory owner or a Highland cattle drover. "That is reassuring," I said, making my voice as cold as the weather outside, "but I would dearly have liked to see you when I was living in terror."

"I am here now," Mr. Kemp pointed out, quite truthfully. "And if you would stop looking for an argument for a moment, I will tell you why."

I stopped at once, for that was the first time Mr. Kemp had ever raised his voice in my presence. "Yes, Mr. Kemp?"

"Your Mr. Forres, John Forres, has declared that he will never stop looking for you. He says that he intends to marry nobody else but you, ever."

It must have been a minute before I could speak. "I had hoped that he would lose interest," I said, faintly.

"It appears not," Mr. Kemp told me.

"Then what are we to do, Mr. Kemp?" I waited for his solution. The cottage that I was in afforded proof of his resilience, and I knew that he would have some plan in mind.

"It appears that Mr. Forres will require some persuasion that you are not the correct woman for his wife."

I agreed.

"So let us persuade him."

"Yes, Mr. Kemp," I attempted to retain my patience. "But how?"

"The solution is simple," Mr. Kemp said. "We get married."

I do not think that I have experienced quite that sensation of joy before, but Mr. Kemp's next words sent me plummeting straight back down.

"Not in reality, of course, our respective social positions would preclude that, but as handfasters."

The word meant nothing to me. "I am sorry Mr. Kemp: I am dumfounded; as what, pray?"

"We get handfasted." Mr. Kemp sat me down and piled some peat on the fire. As I sat there he explained. "Handfasting is a form of trial marriage that some of the … lower … orders use in Scotland. A man and woman declare themselves married for a period of a year, and after that, they could decide whether to legitimise the relationship with a proper wedding or shake hands and go their separate ways."

I saw the obvious flaws. "So you can use me as a wife," I said deliberately crude, "and then, when I am forever sullied, wave goodbye and find somebody else?"

Mr. Kemp's smile was as infuriatingly understanding as ever. "Don't you trust me? It's not that long since you said that you loved me."

That was true, and a year was a long time. I closed my eyes, contemplating a handfasted year with Willie Kemp. What could be finer, I thought and smiled across to him. A year with the man that I loved, a year in which John Forres would certainly lose interest, 365 days to convince Mr. Kemp that I was the best woman for him. And the same number of nights of course.

"I probably trust you more than any man I have ever met," I said. That was true. For goodness sake, it was only a few minutes since I had been prancing about naked in front of this man, and he had acted as a complete gentleman. Or as a man with no interest in me at all.

That thought made me sit up straight.

"Mr. Kemp," I spoke so quietly that he must have heard the sudden hammer of my heart. "Please answer me one simple question."

He took a step back, suddenly wary. "That depends entirely on the nature of the question."

I took a deep breath. "Mr. Kemp," I said. "Do you care for me? Even if only a little?"

Mr. Kemp looked relieved. I suspect he thought I was going to propose, or ask for financial help. "Miss Lamont. I do care for you. I am not in the habit of kissing women for whom I care nothing."

Now, you may think that his statement was so obvious that I could ignore it, but when somebody you love declares even a basic liking for you, it makes you extremely elated.

"Then let us get handfasted," I said, still unsure what the procedure entailed.

Mr. Kemp looked at me and smiled. "Even when I am only a mere artisan and you are a gentlewoman born and bred?"

"I do not care!" I told him. I still do not know why I fell in love with that awkward man, but I did, then, and that is an end to it. "I love you, not your station in life! Maybe if we go home married, mother might find you a suitable job. Maybe you could work as an engineer on the estate, or be a factor, or even an estate commissioner. I don't know."

Mr. Kemp smiled. "Thank you for the thought," he said, "but I would prefer to remain in my own area." He looked down at me from his great height. "Perhaps you will get used to my type of life."

I thought, appalled, of a lifetime of such hardships as I had endured in the tiny cottage and was about to shake my head, but then I thought of a lifetime shared with Willie Kemp. "Perhaps I will, as long as you do not leave me alone again for such a long period of time."

His smile broadened. "I promise that I will never leave you alone again for such a long period of time," he said, solemnly. "And now, if you are sure that you agree, let us get handfasted."

"How?" I was suddenly afraid. "I do not know what to do. I have never heard of such a thing until this very minute."

Mr. Kemp looked around the room, with its plain furniture and my clothes drying beside the bright fire. "First we will need a couple of witnesses," he told me, "and we will find somewhere suitable to perform the ceremony."

I looked at him with his slow smile and the deep humour behind those dark brown eyes. Somehow I knew that Willie Kemp was playing a devious game with me, but for the life of me I could not work out what. I thought that I could trust him, but perhaps his apparent refusal to take advantage of me was itself a ruse? Was he luring me into a position where I was completely at his mercy? All the years of reading Gothic novels, where every man is either a brave hero or a blatant villain, had taken their toll on my young mind.

I hesitated.

Could I really trust this man with everything I had left?

Chapter Ten

"Well?" Mr. Kemp extended a hand in invitation. "Shall we?"

That was really my last chance. I could have said no and still returned to my old life. Mr. Kemp had told me that, despite my recent behaviour and tattered reputation, John Forres still wanted me as his wife, so I could have all the clothes, dances, balls and security that any woman would desire, or I could head for love with this enigmatic mechanic and live in poverty beyond the fringes of society.

Was I tempted? Of course, I was, but not for long. And nor would you be, my dears, not as a healthy, red-blooded eighteen- year- old with all a young girl's hopes and desires running through your body.

"Of course we shall," I took hold of his hand and allowed him to lead me into a life of hardship and poverty.

According to Mr. Kemp, we needed two witnesses and a length of twine for a proper handfasting ceremony. I had no idea where we could find any of these items, but Mr. Kemp took me out of my cottage and into the snowy hills. I could not see where the paths were in that white sameness, but Mr. Kemp had no difficulty as he led me by devious tracks to a second cottage about two miles away and overlooking a crooked village.

"That is Carlops," he told me. "The name comes from the Carlin's Loup, the witches leap, or so the old folk say."

I looked down upon the straggle of weaver's cottages where the roofs were free of snow and the clatter of the looms was a constant companion, and I wondered about the life of the people who lived there. Perhaps someday Mr. Kemp would find us a cottage in a place like that. After my solitary abode in the hills, it seemed quite attractive. "Wait here, please." Leaving me in a sheltered dell, where birch trees displayed their silver bark and a grassy banking eased the bite of the wind, Mr. Kemp slipped softly down to Carlops. He returned within a few minutes, bringing with him a man who might have been forty, but who looked more like a gaberlunzie beggar than a respectable gentleman, with his clothes tattered and tobacco stains in his ragged beard.

"This is Ebeneezer Linton," Mr. Kemp announced, "and a more honest fellow you would be hard pressed to find."

I looked at the ragged apparition and tried to smile, but all the time I wondered at the low company into which I had fallen. "Oh mother," I thought to myself, "please do not ever find out about your daughter's misbehaviour down in the south country."

"Hello, young Alison!" Ebeneezer gave a gap-toothed grin. "Willie told me that he was getting handfasted rather than a common marriage. Aye," he eyed me up and down, nodding all the while, "you're a choice piece. He's got a good eye for a woman, has our Willie."

I nodded, trying not to allow the horror to show in my face. That this rough blackguard should address me so familiarly was bad enough, but that he should call me a 'choice piece' as though I were some animal in the market! John Forres may have been arrogant, but he was never impolite. Besides, the man's accent was so strong that I barely understood a syllable.

"Never mind Ebenezer's words," Mr. Kemp advised. "He's a wee bit rough but sound at bottom. Just one more call to make and we'll be ready."

There was another trail over these barren white hills, with the wind biting through my cloak and my two companions talking quietly about machinery and levers and such like subjects. Again I wondered if I was making the correct choice, but when Willie Kemp guided me over the many churning burns, his touch was as gentle as a dove. All the roughness was outward, I believed, and I walked onward with romance overcoming any shred of sense that I may have had.

People will tell you that love conquers all, dears, but don't you believe it. This life requires a hard head as much as a tender heart, and life without both is out of balance. Surely, aim for the man you love, but don't throw away all your assets in the pursuit of a foolish dream. Keep a foot in both camps until you are totally sure, and then leap for him, thrust in your nails and cling for dear life, for there is bound to be somebody willing to take him away.

If I had thought that Ebeneezer Linton looked like a sorner, the next witness would have made Old Hornie cower and back away. Mr. Kemp took me to a gypsy encampment deep in the southern hills, where horses shivered in the snow, three battered waggons were spread beneath a copse of shivering elder trees and a group of tanned people looked up. I backed away from the barking dogs until an old woman shambled along, the rings in her ears dangling almost to her unwashed neck and her eyes as bright and hard as Aunt Elspeth's diamonds.

"Is that you, Willie Kemp?"

"It is, Mother Faa." Mr. Kemp bowed respectfully.

"Aye, so it is, so it is. But who is this with you?" Mother Faa peered from within the tawdry rags that nearly concealed her sharp face.

"This is Ebeneezer."

"Oh, I know Ebeneezer Linton. I knew his father's father before his grandmother ever did. Who is the other one?" Her claws tugged at my cloak as she peered into my face. "The pretty one."

"This is Alison Lamont."

"Ah; a girl from the Highlands." The old hag grinned, showing perfect white teeth. "I can smell the Gael in you," she told me. "And what are you doing so far from home?"

The question was directed to me, and I answered as honestly as I could. "Mr. Kemp and I are to be handfasted. He requires that you should be a witness."

"Does he indeed?" Mother Faa did not ease her scrutiny, pulling back my cloak to gaze at what could be seen of my shape. "Aye, I see why. You have a plump body and fine, childbearing hips."

Stepping back, I would have closed by cloak had she not gripped like the devil himself. "I would be much obliged, madam if you could refrain from such personal observations."

Mother Faa placed one hand against my stomach. "Ebeneezer Linton has buried two wives and has seventeen children," she told me, "so he has no interest in a child such as you, while Willie Kemp has brought you here for my approval. Is that not so, Willie?"

I shuddered, wondering what sort of man would subject his intended to an inspection by such an old witch as this.

Mother Faa chuckled, tapped my stomach lightly and carefully replaced my cloak. "You have nothing to worry about there, Willie. In any respect."

"I did not think I had, Mother Faa," Mr. Kemp said quietly.

I looked at him. "Mr. Kemp! How dare you treat me so! You have no right!"

"And she has fire!" Mother Faa ignored my outburst quite as much as did Mr. Kemp. "You two will have such exciting arguments. I nearly envy you the joy of discovering each other."

Mr. Kemp smiled again. "Thank you, Mother Faa," he said, "and now perhaps, we may proceed to the proper place?"

"Not yet," I said. I knew that I could not alter what had happened, but I demanded fairness, at least. "If I am to be examined, then so should Mr. Kemp!"

Mother Faa looked at me with amusement in those hard eyes, and Ebeneezer laughed out loud.

"She certainly has all the spirit you will need," Mother Faa said, "and she is right. The gander must share the sauce of the goose!"

I watched, feeling justified as the old gypsy opened Mr. Kemp's jacket and pawed him in the same manner as he had me. Of course, I did not believe a word that she said, for she had probably known

Mr. Kemp for years, but at least I had shown that I was not to be tri-fled with.

"He has a fine body, Miss Lamont," Mother Faa told me, "but you have already seen it."

How in the Lord's name did she know that?

Her chuckle would not have been out of place in Weir the Wiz-ard's house. I saw her delve further down and secretly rejoiced at Mr. Kemp's involuntary wince. "Oh yes, Miss Lamont, everything is in order. He will make a fine husband." Her final cackle brought a blush to Mr. Kemp's face and caused Ebeneezer to laugh out loud. "He is untried, however."

"That will do, Madam." I pulled the old hag's hand from its personal probing. "You have told us quite enough."

Appearing not quite as confident as he had been only a few mo-ments before, Mr. Kemp led us back to the hills, unerringly following a succession of sheep paths that I could not see. He seemed to know his way by some instinct and eventually brought us to the grey cairn that surmounted Harper's Hill. Perhaps it was the wind that had removed the cover of snow on that high and windy place, or perhaps old Mother Faa had something to do with it: I rather suspected the latter.

"Here we are." Mr. Kemp said, not even out of breath, although I was panting like a pair of bellows and Ebeneezer was about half a mile be-hind and labouring mightily. Old Mother Faa was walking alongside us as if she were floating on air, which she probably was, the evil old witch.

You will all know what a cairn is, my dears, but maybe you have never seen the cairn on Harper's Hill? It is large, taller than a man, and composed of different sizes of stone, large and small all jumbled together higgledy- piggledy. The historical people tell us that some ancient chief is buried underneath, but God alone knows why they went to such trouble to get rid of a man who was probably a rogue anyway. Maybe they were making sure he stayed down by piling as much weight on top of him as possible.

But that day such metaphysical thoughts did not concern me in the slightest. After so much hardship, and enduring the company of two creatures who would have been far better locked in bedlam than loose with respectable people, I was about to become handfasted to Mr. Kemp.

"So what do we do?" I asked and was surprised when Mr. Kemp shook his head.

"I'm not sure," he said. "I've never been handfasted before. That's why I chose these two. Ebeneezer was handfasted once, and Mother Faa knows everything about everything."

I nodded; I should have realised that there was some logic in Mr. Kemp's choice. "Mr. Linton," I addressed the tattered Ebeneezer. "Did you marry your handfasted wife?"

"Good Lord no," he seemed to recoil at the very suggestion. "I did not marry that one. We fell out after a few weeks and went our separate ways." He nodded, "that is what the whole idea is about, a trial marriage to find out if you are suitable. It was entertaining while it lasted, though." His eyes brightened with the memory.

Not in the slightest reassured by the story of collapse, I hoped that Mother Faa would be more encouraging.

"Up on the cairn," she ordered. "That's the place. Start at the top."

"And from there it's all downhill," Ebeneezer chuckled. "I still see my daughter, though."

That simple statement appalled me. I had not considered having children, and outside wedlock too. "She would be illegitimate!" I said in horror.

"And none the less welcome for that," Ebeneezer revealed a humanity that I found surprising in one so rough.

Mr. Kemp gave me his slow smile. "The question of children is something that Miss Lamont and I can work out between us," he said. "It is surely the concern of nobody else."

The day remained fair as we scrambled to the summit of that cairn and, despite the oncoming ceremony; I admired the view spread before me. From up there I could see the entire Pentland range, fold upon fold of brilliant white hills, dotted with shivering sheep and scattered with trees and the smoke from cottages. I could see the hope in which my own cottage was situated, and the distant Firth of Forth, where tiny white specks revealed the passage of ships.

I could also see the spread of Edinburgh under its permanent reek of smoke and the distinctive rock on which the castle stood. For a moment I thought of my comfortable bedroom in George Street, and the bustle of servants, and Aunt Elspeth's efficient serenity, and Louise's sulky face, and I wished that I was there.

"Are you ready?" Mother Faa poked a hard finger into my ribs and I looked toward Willie Kemp, standing with the wind tousling his hair and his cloak battered and mud- stained, and I wondered anew if I should swap the life to which I belonged for a man of whose love I was doubtful.

Opening my mouth to say no, I said "of course" as soon as I saw the smile in Mr. Kemp's eyes, and after that, it was too late to object.

"Hold hands, then," Mother Faa said. Although she was the oldest of any of us by some years, she seemed completely at ease up on that windy cairn, and gave her orders as if by right.

Mr. Kemp held out his hand at once, and I took hold. His grip was warm and strong and, I was glad to note, completely devoid of grease or oil. Presumably, he had washed especially for the ceremony.

"Do you both swear to be loyal and faithful to each other, from this day until this a year and a day from now?"

Mother Faa's words sounded archaic as if they had been created many centuries ago. I wondered how many couples had heard them, and how many had bound themselves by the same promise.

"I do," Mr. Kemp said, strongly.

"I do," I repeated, surprised that my voice was firm, unlike the erratic thunder of my heart.

"So now." Mother Faa nodded to Ebeneezer. "Tie fast their hands."

To judge by his foolish grin, Ebeneezer had been waiting for just this minute. Hauling a length of twine from his pocket, he lumbered forward and wrapped it around both our wrists, tying us together with a neat bowline.

"There you are now," Mother Faa sounded satisfied. "That is you both handfasted. Now you can do anything that man and wife can do, and nobody can separate you save yourselves."

"Excellent," Dipping into his pocket, Mr. Kemp produced a knife and sliced through the twine. "We no longer need the symbolism, Miss Lamont. We are now together. How do you feel?"

I considered the question as I made my way down to shelter in the lee of the cairn. "I have never felt happier"

I looked across to him and gave a hesitant smile. The entire ceremony had taken only a few minutes, yet it had changed my life completely. I was unsure whether to cry that I could never go back to my old world, or laugh that I had captured Willie Kemp for a year. As you know, my dears, at the age of 18, a year is a long time and I was quite unable to see any further.

Willie Kemp stood on the top of the cairn, looking for the entire world like a Greek God with his broad shoulders and dark hair. Behind him, clouds gathered their forces above the hills, foretelling of the storm to come.

He looked so tall and distant that all my fears returned; we were from different worlds, him and me. While I knew about balls and fashion, music and embroidery and household accounts, he was a man of his hands. While I spoke with gentlemen and ladies and knew how to conduct myself in the great houses of the country, Mr. Kemp knew the servant's quarters and gypsy encampments. What had we in common to make even a handfasted marriage work?

He turned slightly and I saw him in profile. Still as handsome as Hercules, but with new lines on his face, and I realised that he too was unsure. He was not quite the confident man I thought.

"Mr. Kemp," I tried to sound reassuring. "It will be all right."

"Will it indeed, Miss Lamont?" He looked down at me once more with his eyes as sombre as a hanging judge. "I just wish that you knew exactly what you were getting yourself into."

"I have handfasted the man that I love," I said, for at the age of eighteen, everything seems to be so simple. "And the man I also intend to marry."

"And you do not care for our differences?" He was not smiling, indeed he looked so serious that I doubted he realised what he had just done.

"Not a whit," I said, truthfully. "And no more should you. But you should say that I have made you the happiest man in the world."

"So you think I should be the happiest man?" Mr. Kemp began to smile again, that same slow smile that I knew signified reassurance. "My dear Miss Lamont, I wish I had your ability to see everything in black and white."

"You can have," I told him, "if you just have trust."

"Well, perhaps you could be right." Mr. Kemp descended from his position at the top of his cairn and clattered to my side. His arm slid around my shoulders. "Shall we get back to our cottage?"

Mr. Kemp's use of that single word 'our' told me he had indeed realised what he had just done. It was not his cottage or my cottage but *our* cottage, and that casual assumption of shared possession marked possibly the most significant statement that Willie Kemp made that afternoon.

"Yes," I said, pushing against his hard body. "We should get back to *our* cottage."

I did not see when Ebeneezer and Mother Faa left us, or where they went, and I did not care, for I was lost within our own world. That afternoon I finally felt that I had come closer to Willie Kemp.

Unfortunately, I did not know the man at all, damn his scheming ways. Now dears, it has been said that you never truly get to know another person, for they always have a hidden side, and that was certainly true of Willie Kemp. He was the first love of my life, as I hope I have made plain, but even that day when we handfasted on top of that windy cairn I could not even have guessed at the depths of his trickery.

But I did not know that yet. He held me close on that carefree walk from Harper Hill to our cottage, and I savoured every single step. If I close my eyes I can still feel the roughness of his cloak on my face and listen to the regular crunch of snow beneath his feet. I can honestly say that I was happier than I had ever been in my life, but the walk was only the beginning.

While we were busy on Harper Hill, one or more of Mr. Kemp's friends had visited our cottage. When I left that morning the room had been drab and dismal, festooned with wet clothing and with the peat barely smouldering in the grate. Now it was bright with holly wreaths and red berries, with tall flames leaping in the fireplace and a table laden with food.

"Your titled friends may go on a honeymoon," Mr. Kemp said, "but we poor people must make do with what we can." He was smiling as he closed the door behind us and lit the two wax candles that had appeared on the table. Until then I had made do with tallow, the stinking butcher's candles scorned by my peers.

"I think that you are rich in friends, Mr. Kemp," I said. The mention of a honeymoon reminded me that, in a way, this was my wedding night, with all that entailed.

"At present," he indicated the laden table, "at least we are rich in food. You will be hungry"

I was. I had eaten sparsely for the past week, and I am a woman who enjoys her food. People who eat alone seldom eat as much as those who relish company, and I was always a gregarious girl. Perhaps that comes from having a large family, but I find solitariness does not come easy, and I was happy to have Mr. Kemp back in our cottage.

I doubt that I stopped talking once during the next hour, except when I was chewing of course, for there is nothing less romantic than talking and eating simultaneously. I have no idea what I said, but I probably gave Mr. Kemp a blow-by-blow account of everything that had happened that past week, every step I had taken and every piece of peat I had placed on the fire.

He listened with that patience that seemed natural to him, either smiling whimsically or looking solemn and supporting, whichever he thought most appropriate to my words at the time.

Every so often I stopped to ask him a question but permitted him only a couple of words before I was off again, rattling my adventures off until the poor man must have been bored to tears. Don't ever bore your men, my dears, for that is a sure way of ensuring they search for something more interesting than your embroidery or Alicia somebody-or-other said to Mrs. Thingamajig or what Mrs. MacDonald's servants were doing with the duck.

It was only when I realised how much I was dominating the conversation that I began to slow down. Mr. Kemp was watching me, his back to the fire and his eyes quizzical; as if he were trying to comprehend this newly handfasted wife of his, and only then did I understand that this was my wedding night.

The fear came suddenly, and, looking back, I can blame nobody but myself. It had been my choice to leave my home, my choice to ask Willie Kemp for help and my choice to agree to the handfasting. Now I was alone in a lonely cottage with this large and rough man. I looked up suddenly and inadvertently stepped back.

"It is all right," Mr. Kemp must have read my fears. He was smiling at me in a manner I had not seen before. He motioned to the chair, "sit down, Miss Lamont, and relax. You are in absolutely no danger from me, but we have a great deal to discuss."

"In no danger, sir?" I was unsure whether to be relieved, annoyed or disappointed. Was Willie Kemp turning me down? Was I not good enough for him? Or perhaps I was not desirable enough? Maybe Mr. Kemp preferred thin women … I could lose weight…

"No." Mr. Kemp shook his head. "You may sleep sound and secure tonight, Miss Lamont."

"But we are handfasted. We are as good as married!" If Mr. Kemp had said I was safe, then I knew that I was indeed safe, which meant that I could shout at him. It is always best to know these things about your men, my dears before you start an argument. "Mr. Kemp, are you not in the slightest bit interested in me?" I tried to recollect his expression when he had walked in on me that morning. Had he been shocked, or disgusted?

"We are handfasted," he agreed, "legally and before witnesses. Nobody can take that from us."

"Mr. Kemp," I said, severely. "What are your intentions?"

He did not reply for a second, so I could distinctly hear the fizz of the fire and smell the sweet perfume of the peat.

"Please tell me." That was more of a plea than a demand, but you see, I was not nearly as certain as I thought. Although I did love this man dearly, I was not secure enough in myself to expect him to love me back. It was more of a hope than anything else.

At last Mr. Kemp sighed and stepped away from the fire. "Miss Lamont," he spoke more slowly than ever, with a serious, lowering expression on his face that I thought betokened trouble. "We have a journey to make."

"What sort of journey, pray?" I looked around the now-friendly cottage where I had expected to spend the first night of my handfasted marriage. Although I was afraid of tonight, I also knew that it would be special, something that I would always remember. After all, Louise had instructed me in the generalities; I knew what went where, at least roughly; I only wanted the particulars and the love of Willie Kemp. "Are you sure, sir?"

He sighed again. "I am very sure, Miss Lamont. We must leave our cottage."

"No!" I refused. There had been so much change in my life that I could not countenance any more.

"One walk," Mr. Kemp promised, "and we will be together."

"We are together now," I wailed, nearly crying, and on my wedding night too.

"One walk," he said, smiling solemnly, "and then I think you will be ... more content."

Of course, I followed him. We left our cottage within ten minutes, with Mr. Kemp calm as he ever was and me huffing and sulking, as I was entitled to, I believe.

Strangely, there were two horses tethered outside, and I looked at Mr. Kemp as he helped me mount and slid on his beast as to the manner born.

"Where did these horses come from Mr. Kemp, and where are we going?"

"Not far," he told me, and smiled again. "Do you trust me?"

"I do," I said, fool that I was ever to trust that man.

The night was brisk and sharp, with the hills hard -edged against the stars and our breath steaming not unpleasantly around our faces. We rode slowly, and Mr. Kemp looked over at me continually, as if to ensure that I had not strayed. As if I would. I had no idea what was about to happen, but I trusted Mr. Kemp. I know that you will find that hard to believe after all that I had already endured, and given the situation in which I am now, but women do trust the men they love.

Damn him and his trickery.

Chapter Eleven

"I know this place!"

Mr. Kemp had stopped on a slight ridge that overlooked a broad valley. There was a dry stone dyke stretching forever in either direction, powdered with frozen snow and with the occasional gate marked by tall stone posts. In front of us, and nestling comfortably in a hollow sheltered by mature trees, was the big house in which I had seen Louise dance only a few nights before.

The house was long and low, only three stories high and built in the most modern neo-classical style, with severe Doric pillars flanking a front door to which a dozen steps made a sweeping entrance. Yellow light gleamed from a score of tall windows, and all around was the aura of wealth and comfort.

"This is Cairnsmuir House," Mr. Kemp told me. "And we are going inside."

"But Mr. Kemp; I do not want to go inside!" Instinctively I glanced down at myself. My clothes had been respectable once, but a week's hard wear in the Pentland Hills had reduced them to something less than beggarly. "I cannot go like this!"

Mr. Kemp, the blackguard, did not wait for my excuses. He was through the gate and riding on, with me trailing behind him, asking questions to which he gave not a single syllable in answer.

"Mr. Kemp! I demand that you tell me what is happening! Mr. Kemp, where are you taking me, and why, and can I please get changed first?"

Of course, I realised that we would be going to the servant's quarters as we had at Bonaly so there was no real need for respectability, but a gentlewoman does like to look her best. Unfortunately, Mr. Kemp seemed to have lost his way so we rode directly to the front door.

"Leave the horses," Mr. Kemp ordered, and walked up the steps.

For an instant, I cringed at the thought that he would demand entrance, but instead, he slipped in a side door that I had not seen, turned, and beckoned for me to join him.

A week in the wilds had altered me.

"I cannot go in there!" The idea shocked me. In all but birth and upbringing and blood, I was a mechanic's wife; I no longer belonged in such a place.

Smiling, Mr. Kemp gently pulled me behind him and closed the door. Now, girls, I had spent my life in and around the houses of the gentry, mainly in Badenoch but also, as you know, in Edinburgh, but I had never seen such an establishment as Cairnsmuir House. I have already indicated that it was not particularly large, but everything in it was absolutely modern. The style was classical, the furniture could have come from the most fashionable salon in Paris and the taste was immaculate. I had thought that Aunt Elspeth was a model for perfection, but Mrs. Cairnsmuir outshone her in every department.

I felt like an intruder in such a place, a gaberlunzie encroaching on a grand duchess, a pauper within a palace. I found that I was literally walking on tip toes as I followed Willie Kemp. We passed through an outer entrance hall, where statues of naked Greek Gods flaunted themselves quite unashamedly and great Corinthian pillars supported a ceiling absolutely covered in Adam's ornate plasterwork when I protested again.

"Mr. Kemp! Where are we going?"

I never did find out, for pandemonium struck us just then.

There was a scream, followed by raised voices, both male and female, and a succession of bangs as doors opened and closed all around. First, one servant appeared, and then another, stared at us and ran hither and thither as though Lucifer himself had ascended from his Pit to lay claim to this earthly paradise that was Cairnsmuir.

"What the devil?" Even calm Willie Kemp joined in the general agitation, grabbing at scurrying servants in his efforts to find out what was happening. "I say there, what's all the commotion?"

At length, Mrs. Cairnsmuir appeared, with my Aunt Elspeth at her side. Both were in a state of flux that I had never imagined possible, and I presumed that they had just caught sight of me in my beggar's rags, and had heard that I was handfasted to a mechanic.

But not a bit of it; the only concern they had was for that lion-hunting minx of a cousin of mine. The name of Louise was on everybody's lips while they barely spared me a glance. I was most put out, as you can imagine, but all my pouting and postulating were in vain. They did not care for the predicament of their relative from Badenoch.

"It's Louise Ballantyne!" Mrs. Cairnsmuir seemed to accept Willie Kemp's presence without a qualm. Indeed, everybody always seemed to accept Willie Kemp. Perhaps, I thought, there is something to be said for eccentricity; nobody expects you to conform, so after a while, nobody cares how you look or when you appear. There must be a lesson in that, somewhere, but at that moment I was far more concerned with their complete disregard for me.

At eighteen, you see, I thought that the entire world revolved around me.

"What about Louise Ballantyne?" Mr. Kemp did not even bother to introduce me, his handfasted wife, to the assembled and very agitated company.

"She's run off!" Mrs. Cairnsmuir grabbed hold of Mr. Kemp's shoulders. "She has eloped with that Frenchman!"

The words shocked me to the core. Of course, I had always known that Louise lacked judgement; that was taken as normal, but to abscond with a Frenchman was going a bit too far. I mean, the French were all republicans that season, and quite beyond the pale of fashionable society. It was all very well for Lady Elspeth or even Mrs. Cairnsmuir to invite a few to a dance now and then, for their positions were secure, but for an unattached gentlewoman to run with one. Well, it made my mismatch seem quite trivial. Trust Louise to steal all the limelight.

"My goodness," I thought, happily, "she will be in trouble when she gets home."

And then I realised that she might not get home. She might run to France, and we would never see her sulky face again.

I saw John Forres in the crowd behind my aunt, looking quite alarmed as he pressed snuff into his left nostril and sneezed most delicately. And then Mrs. Cairnsmuir was speaking again.

"Willie Kemp." Her hands were firm on his shoulders. "You must chase after them. They have been gone less than an hour, so you may catch them yet."

"Tell me more," Mr. Kemp asked. He seemed the calmest person there, for I was all a-flutter at the excitement, the servants were screaming and chattering like a cage load of monkeys and Aunt Elspeth looked fit to swoon.

"I must know more," Mr. Kemp insisted. "What horses are they riding, and what are they wearing. What road did they take? Where are they headed?"

I saw Mrs. Cairnsmuir take a deep breath in a visible effort to calm herself down. "Of course," she said, and released Mr. Kemp's shoulders. I thought it strange that she should ask him for help, but then I realised that there was nobody else. Women could not chase a pair of runaways, servants had no authority and John Forres was a broken reed, already reaching for a chair in which to rest after the shock.

"They have taken my green gig, so they may make good speed."

Willie Kemp nodded. "That was eminently sensible of them. It is fast, and Miss Ballantyne would not ride well at night. In what direction have they gone, pray?"

"They took the Edinburgh road. I fear they may take ship tomorrow."

"I see." Mr. Kemp nodded. "Well, I shall endeavour to head them off tonight, before they reach the city." He glanced over his shoulder and spoke the first words that had been directed toward me since the excitement started. "Miss Lamont, I fear you must fend for yourself tonight. Never fear, you are safe here."

That was twice that Mr. Kemp had assured me that I was safe. "Thank you for your concern, Mr. Kemp," I said, tartly, "but I think that my place is by your side."

For a moment I thought that he was going to push me away, but with a glance at Mrs. Cairnsmuir, he nodded and gave the most devil may care grin I had ever seen in my life. "I do believe that it is," he said. "Can you keep up?"

"I've been riding since before I could walk," I told him. I did not tell him that for the first ten years of my life it was on Highland garrons, but the rough terrain of Badenoch would surely make up for the horse's lack of height.

"Come on then, Miss Lamont," he said, and with hardly a nod to Aunt Elspeth or a by-your-leave to Mrs. Cairnsmuir, he had dragged me to the stable block behind the house.

That too was in an uproar, with stable boys and grooms and God-knows-whats all running around frantically, no doubt enjoying the commotion. Everybody loves a good scandal, as long as they are not directly involved, and my cousin Louise had certainly given the Cairnsmuir household something to keep them occupied that January of 1812. My goodness though, but did they not jump when Mr. Kemp asked them to saddle two horses? I have never seen such instant respect.

"Side saddle or plain?" Mr. Kemp glanced at me and answered his own question. "Side saddle, but can you ride fast like that?"

I could not, but I had never ridden astride. It's damnably unfair, you know, that women are restricted in so many things. However, we do have other advantages that men do not even know about.

Within ten minutes we had left the stables behind and were trotting down the frosty drive that led to the Edinburgh Road. Mrs. Cairnsmuir followed, calling out advice, while Aunt Elspeth merely watched, both hands twisting her shawl while her mouth was working silently. For a moment I felt sorry for her; one of the girls in her care had run off with a Frenchman and the other was handfasted to a mechanic. What a failure she had proved and all her best friends would enjoy assassinating her character and morals until the next scandal happened along.

Now in my day, the roads fringing the Pentland Hills were rough and ready and there were still tolls to slow down traffic and provide a nuisance. I followed at Mr. Kemp's heels, getting used to the feel of my horse as I rode. She was a powerful brute, a piebald mare with a hard mouth and strong flanks, so I had to use bit and spurs to control her and even wielded the whip on occasion, which is something I am loath to do.

"Are you ready?" Mr. Kemp looked across at me, his eyes urgent and impatience in the set of those broad shoulders. I can see him now, silhouetted against the star-lit night, with the hills behind him and the snow beginning to whirl in great white flakes that settled, unmelting, on our cloaks.

"I'm ready;" I had the measure of the horse, I was comfortable in the saddle and the reputation of my cousin was at stake. What an adventure!

Touching spurs to his horse, Mr. Kemp increased our speed steadily until we were cantering along that frosty road, with the horse's hooves drumming noisily and the great bare hills drifting past. Now, you girls have never experienced the excitement of a moonlight gallop, I hope, and you will probably never know the true thrill of horseback riding. Not as a sport or a hobby, but as a way of life. These railway trains and comfortable stage coaches have taken away much of the fun in life, for when we did things, they mattered. And that frantic ride really mattered.

Once he started, Mr. Kemp did not relent, and we pushed on, passing the village of Linton Roderick and the lovely house of Newhall; Carlops, with its memories of Ebeneezer, Nine Mile Burn with its dark inn and the tiny hamlets of Silverburn and Howgate. The miles flowed past in a blur of foaming horses and skill, for we had to really ride. The road was snowy, you see, with patches of ice, and we had no light but that provided by nature's lantern.

I followed Mr. Kemp's directions, obeying his instructions implicitly as he showed me a dangerous stretch of ice or the best route to take, but I kept up. I am proud to say that I did not lag behind so when we reached the outskirts of Edinburgh I was only a few yards behind, but our horses were completely blown.

"Look," Mr. Kemp indicated the road ahead. Until now it had been white with new-blown snow, but he showed me the distinct mark of a carriage, with the prints of four hooves and the straight grooves of two large wheels. "That's their gig, I'll bet my life on it."

"Can we catch them?" I did not doubt Mr. Kemp's word. If he said that Louise's gig had made these marks, then I accepted that he was correct.

"Perhaps we may, Miss Lamont. How is your horse?" Mr. Kemp looked closely at me. "More importantly, how are you?"

I was tired but exhilarated. This mad moonlight dash with Mr. Kemp was something I would always treasure. We do so love to store these memories, don't we? And we think that such adventures bring people together in love, but that is not the case, my dears. Love is more than a few hours of adventure or an hour or so of abandoned passion and exposed flesh. Love is the day to day grind of life, of living together through bad times and good, of bringing up children, of surviving the disappointments and triumphs and pain of life and still being together and happy in each other's company. That makes a true marriage, girls, not these mad cap escapades.

They do provide the most splendid memories though.

"Keep up as best you can, Miss Lamont." Mr. Kemp was back in the saddle and pushing his horse through the fringes of Edinburgh, with me riding at his side with my hair a wind blasted shambles and my face raw red.

I said that women do have some advantages that men do not consider, and our weight is one. Now, we had been riding for exactly the same length of time, but while Mr. Kemp's horse was gasping and shivering, mine was good for another few miles. Why was that? Why, simply because I am the lighter rider. True, I was not the most slender of girls, for even then my curves were ample, but even so, I weighed much less than Mr. Kemp.

Edinburgh has expanded since my day, with new suburbs and streets in every direction, so you must imagine it as little more than the Auld Town and the graceful New. There was a scattering of villas beyond the boundaries, but many of the little villages that are now incorporated within the burgh were then country hamlets, while Leith was connected to the capital by the broad street of the Walk and very little else.

Within ten minutes we were riding along the quiet streets with the grey buildings on either side, their blank windows staring accusingly at us and only a few late night pedestrians wondering who we were and what we were doing. Unfortunately, even when quiet, Edinburgh possessed more wheeled traffic than most places in Scotland, and the marks of Louise's gig were soon lost in the general confusion.

"They've gone," Mr. Kemp said, and for only the second time since I had met him, he resorted to very commonplace language.

"Mr. Kemp," I ignored his impropriety. After all, he was only a mechanic and we must make allowances. "You have traced them this far. In your best judgement, where do you think they will go?"

He looked at me, his face drawn. "I was about to ask you the same question," he said. "You know Louise far better than I. Does she have any friends in the city?"

I thought for a few minutes. "Louise has many acquaintances but few friends," I said. "And I cannot think of anybody to whom she could honestly turn in times of trouble."

That was true. Everybody liked Louise on first acquaintance, but her constant comparisons and readiness to criticise always proved wearisome. After a few short hours, people preferred her absence to her company. Poor Louise, so beautiful, so shapely yet so unloved. I felt sorry for her then and resolved to do everything in my power to gain her back. She would have hated to be the wife of a republican anyway; it would be too common for her.

"So then, they could either find an inn or..." Mr. Kemp looked at me with an expression so horrified that I almost screamed. "Or they are going direct to a ship."

"Oh no." I shook my head. "You can't let them sail away, Mr. Kemp. You must stop them."

He was riding even before the last word had left my lips, and I had to use the whip on my poor piebald to catch him. We trotted through Edinburgh's dark streets with our hooves ringing on the cobbles and the jingling of bit and bridle echoing from the serene squares. Without a pause, we passed over the North Bridge, that windy connection between the Old Town and the New; skirted the eastern edge of Princes Street and slithered down the slope to Leith Walk.

You will know the Walk, with its broad street lined with tenements and shops? Well, we pushed our horses down there as if they were fresh young things rather than the tired old nags that they were, but by the time we reached the foot of the Walk, they were completely done.

"We'll have to leave the horses," Mr. Kemp said. He sounded agitated now, in this dark port of stone buildings and interesting nautical smells.

"Mrs. Cairnsmuir won't be pleased," I told him. I had the greatest respect for Mrs. Cairnsmuir, with her icy common sense and level eyes.

"The horses don't count beside the honour of Miss Ballantyne."

I wondered how a mechanic would know anything about honour, but Mr. Kemp seemed to know something about everything.

"Are you sure they will be here?" I looked around at the dark, unlit streets, where huddled people lurched from doorways and somebody was singing a song full of extremely maritime words. My aunt would not have approved of her beloved daughter wandering in such a place. My mother would have had a fit with her leg in the air.

"It's high tide in an hour," Mr. Kemp told me, "and there are a couple of neutral ships ready to sail."

The words meant little to me then, but I have since discovered that Napoleon Bonaparte had established what he called his Continental System, which closed all the ports of Europe to British ships. That meant that only very fast blockade runners and a few ships from ports not at war traded with both Britain and Europe. If there were neutral ships in Leith harbour, then it was virtually certain that they would be sailing to Europe, and Louise and her French companion may well be on board.

I moved on, staggering with fatigue for I had been on the move since just after dawn. Mr. Kemp was quick to support me.

"Go on," I ordered, "leave me behind and save Louise."

"I'm not leaving you," Mr. Kemp said with his arm around my shoulders and his concerned face a foot away from mine.

"But Louise…"

"You're worth a hundred Louises," Mr. Kemp told me. "And I would not leave a dog here, yet alone you."

At that moment the words did not mean much, but I think that was Mr. Kemp's way of declaring his affection for me.

I believe it has altered since, but I thought Leith a dark place of wynds and tall stone buildings, with a plethora of warehouses and grimy beer shops. I followed Mr. Kemp as he hurried to the harbour, where, along a stretch of river he called the Shore, a line of ships was berthed beneath a tall round tower.

"Over there!" Mr. Kemp pointed, and I saw, standing forlorn, a dark gig with a drooping, steaming horse.

"Louise!" I screamed the name, but the only reply came from wailing seagulls. "Louise! Please answer!" I was not surprised when she did not, but somebody in the nearest ship advised me to keep quiet or he would quieten me himself. He used some other words too, but I think they must have been very nautical for I did not recognise them.

"Hello!" Mr. Kemp shouted, and a squat man in a dark uniform appeared. For a moment I thought he was from the Royal Navy and had a terrifying vision of Mr. Kemp being press-ganged, never to be seen again, but it seemed that the squat man was only a Customs officer.

"Did you see the driver of that gig?"Mr. Kemp shot out the question.

The customs man shone a lantern at Mr. Kemp, and then at me, before turning a slow eye to the gig. "Oh yes, there was a man and a woman." He nodded. "Nice looking lassie, she was. She had lovely blonde hair."

"That's her," I confirmed as if there would be a number of young women running loose along the Shore that January night. "That's Louise. Do you know where she is now?" I looked at the waiting ships as if she would magically appear.

Again the man checked me with his lantern. "Aye," he said again. "Her man took her on board *Potomac*."

The name meant nothing to me, but Mr. Kemp started. "And where is *Potomac*, pray?"

Pulling a silver watch from somewhere, the man peered at the dial, looked up and extended a finger upward. "She left on the high tide, about fifteen minutes since, so, given this wind, I'd say she's in the lee of Inchkeith."

Mr. Kemp translated for me. "Louise and the Frenchman are on *Potomac*, that's an American vessel. They left about half an hour ago, so they are out in the Firth of Forth."

I felt my stomach slide sickeningly. For the first time, I wondered what Aunt Elspeth had felt when I disappeared with Willie Kemp. "Then we're lost. She's gone."

"Gone?" the customs man looked curious, but we both ignored him.

I leant against the great stone building at my back. My cousin had run off with a Frenchman and was being taken away to France. There was nothing I could do to save her.

Mr. Kemp, of course, was not so easily defeated. "What way's the wind?" He licked his finger and held it in the air. "Backing easterly," he said, "and the Forth is not an easy waterway to leave."

"She's a right bitch with the wind like this," the Customs man said, pleasantly.

"Then we have a chance!" Mr. Kemp slammed his right fist into the palm of his left hand. "By God! We could not have a better chance!"

The Customs man looked to me and shrugged his shoulders. He obviously doubted Mr. Kemp's sanity; a sentiment that I shared.

"We have a better chance for what, pray?" I asked, slightly hesitantly.

"We have a better chance to catch them, of course! In my steamboat."

Chapter Twelve

I must have stared at that mad man for a full ten seconds. I had vivid memories of scuttling crabwise across the North Loch in that contraption, with various bits and pieces breaking every few minutes and a mocking straggle of spectators. I could not contemplate venturing into the less-than-sheltered waters of the Firth of Forth in such a device.

"Is your boat not on the Nor' Loch?" I knew that there was relief in my voice.

"One of my boats is." Mr. Kemp told me, "the experimental one. The other, my older and more reliable model, is only a few hundred yards from here."

"You have two of such monstrosities?" The next words escaped before I could help myself. "God save us from such tomfoolery!"

Mr. Kemp only smiled. "Such tomfoolery may yet save your cousin." He looked hard at me. "However, I will need help, and Ebeneezer, my crewman, is not here. Will you help me find a suitable replacement?"

That was the first time that Mr. Kemp had asked me for help, and I was unsure whether to be pleased or insulted. Again, I spoke before I thought. "And what is wrong with me? You may recall that I have helped you on a previous occasion."

"You?" Mr. Kemp frowned, and his mouth gaped open. I could nearly hear his mind working as he considered his options. He was standing on the Shore at Leith, with a line of ships moored mizzen to bowsprit and with only the Customs Officer and a woman for company. He had resolved to save Louise from her French prisoner of war, and he had a steam boat, but no crew. What could he do?

"Me," I confirmed, already regretting my rashness.

"Are you willing to sail out there?" Mr. Kemp nodded to the blackness beyond the Shore and I looked out.

Brought up in Badenoch, I knew the Highland hills, and I was beginning to feel more comfortable in Edinburgh, but the sea was a mystery. I had barely been to the coast, yet alone ventured out at night in a contraption that steered crabwise and worked by lumps of coal. I looked at Willie Kemp, bit my fear and nodded. "I will go if you want me to."

His smile was different, not slow but uncertain. "You're a brave woman, Alison."

I had become Alison; not Miss Lamont. Hearing my own name was worth the fear. "So why are we wasting time, Mr. Kemp? My cousin is out there."

The steam boat sat in its own berth in a quiet corner of the harbour, dwarfed by the tall sailing ships on either side. I had expected Mr. Kemp's two boats to be similar, but this one was about twenty feet long, with a taller funnel and two paddle wheels in the stern. There was a wooden ship's wheel about half way down the length, and a massive boiler taking up most of the rest of the space. The name *Mary* was emblazoned in white letters against her blue hull.

"That's my middle name," I pointed out.

"I know," Mr. Kemp said, without offering an explanation, and lent me his hand so I could step on board.

Now, that may sound very gallant and I am well aware that there are a few women today who complain about such acts of chivalry. However, in my day, and even now, women's clothing does not aid active movement. Long skirts and layers of petticoats are not conducive to agility, so Mr. Kemp's hand was very welcome, but he had no real need to cling to me for a long, luxurious second after I boarded *Mary*. Not that I objected of course, but I did think we would be better to hurry after my wayward cousin.

"We'll have to wait until we build up steam," Mr. Kemp spoke as if I knew what he was talking about, "but that won't take too long."

Once Mr. Kemp shovelled fuel into the furnace, he fiddled with his levers and nodded to me. "Get used to the feel of the wheel," he said, "because you'll be steering."

"What?' I stared at him in disbelief. 'I can't steer a boat, Mr. Kemp! I do not have the skill!"

"Would you rather shovel coal?"

The spokes of the wheel were cold and hard in my hands, but it spun easily, and once Mr. Kemp decided that we were ready and cast off the securing lines, I felt the little boat buck under my hands.

"Ease her round slowly," Mr. Kemp sounded quite anxious. "Pretend that she's a prime team, a quality equipage."

The comparison helped a little. This vessel was only a vehicle, like a coach but floating. I turned the spokes.

"You're steering too fast!" Mr. Kemp was quite abrupt.

"I'm sorry," I said, turning the wheel just as hard the opposite direction so the vessel's blunt bow made solid contact with the sea wall.

"Let me," Mr. Kemp dropped his shovel with a clatter and leaped beside me. It was the closest contact I had experienced for some time as he put his hands over mine and very gently eased the wheel around. "Hold her like that," he said, and stepped aside, brushing against me as he pushed a small brass lever that was attached to the boiler.

The steam boat seemed to lurch forward, and those great paddles in the stern moved slowly, churning up the water far more effectively than the boat on the Nor' Loch ever did.

"Steer for the harbour entrance," Mr. Kemp advised and pointed out the lights that marked the space.

Until that second I had enjoyed the thrill of close contact with Mr. Kemp and the excitement of doing something completely different, but now the sea began to kick, *Mary* rode high on a wave and swooped down and I realised exactly what I was doing.

If I had been with anybody else I believe that I would have panicked, but Mr. Kemp had an assurance about him that other men lack. I could draw strength just by looking at him, while one touch of his hand steadied my nerve. Oh, I am not saying he was perfect, far from it, the devious, tricky blackguard, but I admit that it was reassuring to have him near.

I was steering a steam boat on to the Firth of Forth at night. The thought was terrifying until Mr. Kemp looked at me. "Keep her steady," he said and lit a few lanterns to show our position to other vessels. Perhaps that was the objective, but having *Mary* lighted up only served to highlight the stygian blackness outside.

All this time, remember, we had the steady thump, swish, thump of the paddle wheels in the background, while the tall funnel overhead erupted greasy smoke that gusts of wind would blow down upon us. However dishevelled I was at the start of that voyage, a few minutes later I must have looked like a Midlothian collier.

"How far are we going?" Although we had barely cleared the harbour I still had to shout above the chunk of the paddles and the increasing howl of the wind around various parts of the ship. Don't ask me what they are called, my dears, I did not know then and I have never been concerned enough to find out since.

"The Customs officer thought *Potomac* would be in the lee of Inchkeith," Mr. Kemp told me. "With this wind, I cannot see her going much further out. With our steam power, we can go against the wind, of course."

Of course, I thought. You should know the Firth of Forth, my dears, that great bite of the sea that separates Edinburgh from Fife. It is about fifty miles long, from the North Sea all the way to Stirling, but narrows considerably a few miles west of Edinburgh. It is not a clear seaway, as the mariners say, but has a considerable number of small islands, some of which are mere rocks, but others are useful to ships, which use them for shelter in bad weather or adverse winds. The largest of these islands is Inchkeith, that ugly, misshapen chunk of rock you can see from Edinburgh.

"How far is that?" I was already beginning to doubt my wisdom in coming out here with the wind screaming around my ears and the smoke a choking cloud all around. Very bad for the complexion, I believe.

"Not far!" Mr. Kemp was jumping around madly, one minute shovelling coal into the furnace so there was constant steam pressure to keep the paddles turning, the next checking his array of levers and buttons and what not, so the boat moved properly. I was very glad to see that *Mary* steered better than her sister in the North Loch. There was no sideways crab-like motion from her, just a steady if slow movement forward. And to add to my discomfort, *Mary* was also making an up and down and sideways movement, as the wind and sea directed.

I was beginning to feel seasick, but swallowed hard. I did not want Mr. Kemp to see my weakness.

"Cross wind!" Mr. Kemp suddenly bellowed in my ear, and before I had time to ask what the devil he was talking about, a blast of wind came from the left, sorry, the larboard side, and rocked the entire boat. We shipped water, with a great wave cascading over the small handrail that was all that separated us from the sea, and then I was soaked as well as sick.

Mr. Kemp was at my side in a second. "Hold on!" He shouted, as his huge hand closed over mine. Together we wrestled *Mary* back on course. "Well done, Alison! Hold her there!"

I am still unsure where it was I was meant to hold her, or exactly what I had done well, but I smiled through my fear, shook away that portion of the Firth of Forth that had descended on my hair and face, and stared determinedly ahead.

I was aware of Edinburgh's lights to starboard, that's the right- hand side to you lands-women, and a scattering of lights that seemed to bob madly everywhere else. There was one fixed white light directly ahead, which Mr. Kemp pointed to.

"That's the lighthouse on Inchkeith," he told me, "steer a good bit to the left, or we'll run onto the island."

"We'll what?" I heard my voice rise in horror. It was bad enough being out here on this boat that rose and fell and clanked and rattled and chunked and spewed out stinking black smoke, but it would be worse to run onto an island.

"Just do what I say!"

I was determined to do exactly what Mr. Kemp said, but I wished, very fervently, that I had taken his advice an hour ago and remained safe on the Shore at Leith. I have often heard people ridicule mariners for their tall tales and hard drinking, but if that experience of mine in the Firth of Forth, a sheltered waterway, mark you, was typical, they earn every penny they make and the stories are all probably true. If I were a seaman, I would never be sober; such was my impression of the hardship of their lives.

At that moment, of course, I was much more concerned with myself that with any number of anonymous seamen. I gripped the spokes of that wheel until my knuckles were white, whimpered as the chilling water washed around my ankles and stifled my screams as *Mary* crashed into waves that seemed to grow larger every moment.

"There!" Mr. Kemp pointed ahead, where the constant beam of the Inchkeith Light showed like the finger of God. "Steer to larboard – left!"

I did so, as best I was able, with Mr. Kemp's hands on top of mine and my clothes sticking sodden to me.

"And there's *Potomac*."

The American vessel was riding light, or at least she seemed to be floating high on top of the waves, with most of her sails furled. There was a full moon that night, and she rode with what seemed a score of lights proclaiming her presence to the world. My cousin was on board that ship, I thought, possibly deep in the embrace of a Frenchman, and unless I rescued her, she might never see Scotland again.

"Louise!" I shrieked, "Louise!"

Mr. Kemp looked at me. "She can't hear you," he said, and then I saw something that has haunted my worst nightmares ever since. I saw a man walk on to the deck of *Potomac*, lift a speaking trumpet and shout an order, whereupon a rush of ragged seamen erupted from somewhere forward and begin to haul on ropes.

Sails sprouted as if by magic, *Potomac* changed shape, her anchor began to rise and she was veering away from us and into the teeth of the easterly wind.

"Bloody fool!" That was the third time that I had heard Mr. Kemp swear, and this time I entirely agreed with him.

"They're sailing away!" I pointed out the obvious.

"They can't sail in this wind!" Mr. Kemp had to shout above the scream of the wind and the chunk of our paddles.

"Mr. Kemp," I said, "we must catch them and save Louise!"

The bulk of the island sheltered us from the worst of the wind, so the seas became calmer, with less spindrift being kicked from the surface of the waves, and the smoke from our funnel behaved less erratically. I took a deep breath and glanced up at Mr. Kemp.

I have said before that he looked like a Greek god, but now I would say he was Poseidon personified. Rain and seawater had plastered his hair to his face and his clothes to his body so he stood in muscular profile, his straight nose and out-thrust chin the epitome of determination. Perhaps I love him before, but now my feelings momentarily altered. Now my dears, I know that we girls are not supposed to share the same physical feelings as men, who are meant to be baser creatures, but that is all nonsense, as you probably already know.

In that moment my feelings for Mr. Kemp were anything but pure and spiritual. I felt what can only be described as animal lust, something that overpowered me without me being able to do anything about it. I knew then that a mere clasping of hands, a brief caress, even a kiss, was not enough. I wanted to be married to this man in every sense of the word, moral, spiritual, legal and, most definitely physically, and at that second I did not care for anything less.

As you know, I had already seen him naked, which had been a very interesting experience, but this was different. It went beyond appreciation of muscles and shape and, well, *admiration* of other things. It was far deeper, far more demanding and so intense that it was almost painful.

"Mr. Kemp," I shouted, and he looked around at me with his eyes wild and his mouth open.

"Mr. Kemp," I repeated. "I love you!"

He grinned back, and suddenly I had no doubts at all. I wanted to be Mrs. William Kemp for ever and ever Amen, to have and to hold, oh yes, most definitely to hold, for richer or poorer, but preferably richer, until death us do part. Except at that moment, death seemed quite close to parting us and I did not relish the experience.

"I love you too," he shouted over the racket of the engine and thud of the paddles, and then we were out of the lee of the island and the full force of the Forth squall hit us.

It was like nothing I have ever experienced before, as if some giant fist had descended from heaven and stirred up the sea, flicking us around as easily as a cat paws a baby mouse.

I saw *Potomac* stagger under the force of the sea; I saw her move sideways and backwards, as one of her sails exploded into shreds of tattered canvas. I saw Mr. Kemp shovel another load of coal into the furnace and turn to me, shouting something just as the mizzen mast of *Potomac* broke, splintering into three separate segments that all scissored into the sea.

"Mr. Kemp!" I screamed, but he was already with me, turning the wheel so we avoided the massive spars that wind and waves propelled toward us, and then we were alongside that American ship as she lurched at an impossible angle.

"Hold on!" Mr. Kemp yelled, and I did so.

I might have fainted, or perhaps my memory of the next few minutes is just faulty, but I cannot exactly recall the correct sequence of events. I do know that Mr. Kemp was shouting and that *Potomac* veered toward the island, and for one heart-stopping moment I thought that she would strike.

I recall yelling "Louise!" and watching as the stern of the American ship sliced past the foaming rocks of Inchkeith, missing by a few yards, and then she was staggering crazily in the Forth with *Mary* chugging around her like a sheepdog nipping the heels of a bull.

The lights of Edinburgh still shone bright to starboard, and across the Forth, there were reciprocal lights on the Fife side as all the little towns and coastal villages lived snugly as we battled the storm. I have heard since that it was not a real storm, merely what the sailors call a 'cap full of wind' but it certainly seemed real enough to me.

Anyway, Mr. Kemp kept *Mary* close enough to *Potomac* for me to see the members of the crew all rushing around doing nautical things, and then we were both in open water, the wind had altered and the Inchkeith light was astern.

"Where are we going?" I asked.

"We're going to hail her," Mr. Kemp told me, "but I doubt they'll listen."

Mr. Kemp was correct. They ignored both Mr. Kemp's stentorian shouts and my high pitched squeals, and then the wind altered again and *Potomac* ran aground.

It was literally, as simple as that. I believe that an hour passed between the ship losing her mizzen mast – that's the one at the back – and her hitting the small island of Fidra, but it might have been ten minutes or half the night. I was far too busy steering and pushing levers and doing exactly what Mr. Kemp ordered to pay any attention to the time.

However, I do know that it was some time in the early morning. I was so tired that I could hardly keep my eyes open and my head had that fuzzy, couldn't-care-less feeling, but Mr. Kemp was still alert and busy. How he did it I do not know, particularly as I have since learned that all men require constant feeding before they can do any sort of work for more than half an hour at a time, but he was still in command when *Potomac* hit.

"Louise!" I yelled and watched in total horror as that once proud ship ran aground. You may know Fidra, but if not, it is a small, evocatively beautiful island only a mile or so from the southern shore of the Forth. It has a small hump, hardly a hill, at either end, and a low-lying neck in the middle, and it was onto this neck that *Potomac* ran. Normally it is a lovely island to look at, but this night its northern coast was a maelstrom of thundering surf and exploding spindrift. *Potomac* seemed to slide onto this narrowest and lowest part, stop with sickening abruptness and then slowly settle onto her side.

"Stand aside." Mr. Kemp was hardly polite as he took control of the wheel and eased as close to the wreck as he could.

I could see a score of figures struggling on board, with one or two trying to leave the ship, and then there was a terrible rending sound and the mainmast tottered and fell. I have never seen anything quite so terrifying in my life as the sight of that ship tearing itself to pieces on the rocky shore of Fidra.

I looked around the firth, hoping for the sight of a sail. "Will somebody help her?"

Mr. Kemp shook his head. "Not in this wind," he said. "There's nobody here but us!"

He was right. Sail powered ships, you see my dears, cannot go directly against the wind. They can angle their sails to go at many different angles, but that one is impossible. Steamboats, however, can, and Mr. Kemp manoeuvred the tiny *Mary* as close as he could to *Potomac* to pick up survivors. Now some had already reached the island, but there was a small group in the stern that seemed reluctant to leave, possibly because of the bits and pieces of spars and such like that were cascading from the remaining mast.

"Keep her there," Mr. Kemp said to me, and I held the wheel as tightly as I could as the sea seemed to push *Mary* from one side to the other while simultaneously bucking her up and down like an unbroken horse.

With all my attention on that wheel, I hardly noticed what Mr. Kemp was doing until I saw him balanced right in the bow of *Mary*, throwing a length of rope to the poor people on *Potomac*. Only when they rushed to it did I see the splash of a colourful dress and realise that there were women amongst them. "Louise!" I shouted, more in hope than expectation, for in the horrendous din of sea and wind and steamboat, my voice could not carry.

A massive wave struck *Potomac* then, and when the spindrift and spray cleared, I saw that Mr. Kemp had crawled, hand over hand, to the stricken ship and was carrying one of the women to the rope. I tried to watch, but *Mary* veered to starboard and I had to fight the wheel, and when next I looked there was nobody on *Potomac* at all.

"Mr. Kemp!" Again my voice was too weak, and I was unsure what to do. Should I remain where I was, or search for Mr. Kemp and Louise? I hesitated, biting my lip until the blood flowed, and then a succession of waves battered *Mary* so I had no time to do anything but keep her bow toward the wind, as Mr. Kemp had instructed.

I was alone at sea in a tiny boat the mechanics of which I did not understand, and my handfasted husband and my cousin had both been drowned just a few yards from me. What should I do? There was no time to cry, and as yet the full horror had not hit me. It did though, later, again and again.

There was another wave, and another and *Mary* shuddered with each impact. I remained stationary, holding the wheel, obeying the last words that Willie Kemp had given me as I thought of life without him.

"I love you, Willie Kemp," I said, and then screamed it hopelessly into the uncaring wind. "I love you, Willie Kemp!"

"I am glad to hear it," the deep voice sounded right at my shoulder.

"What?" I spun around, nearly letting go of the wheel. "Where have you been and how dare you scare me like that!" Unsure whether to slap him or hug him, I compromised with a loving glare, and then I saw that he was soaked to the skin and carried something over his shoulder.

It was a woman's body, long and blonde haired, and he laid it down gently before kneeling on top. "That's us," Mr. Kemp shouted. "I've released the line so take us out of here as fast as you can!"

By now I knew that the boat required delicate handling so I eased her away from the wreck of *Potomac* and watched as Mr. Kemp vigorously massaged life back into Louise. She sat up, coughing sea water, and stared at me.

"Alison? What are you doing here?" And then we both began to cry.

Chapter Thirteen

I had nightmares about that night for years afterwards. I often woke up, staring into the darkness of the bedroom, shouting the name of Willie Kemp until my husband, your dear, dear great grandfather, would stir, mutter softly and usually tell me to go back to sleep. Sometimes, though, he would sit up beside me and hold me tight and offer comfort and a friendly ear as I remembered the terrors of that night.

But to continue with my tale...

Crying did not help, of course, and I soon had to leave Louise lying a blonde heap on the deck and run around at the orders of the tyrannical Mr. Kemp. I did not like to neglect my troublesome cousin, but what would you? If I continued to caress her, *Mary* would have run afoul of Fidra, or turned turtle, or blown up, or met some other nautical fate, so I am afraid Louise had to attend to her herself while I did the needful with the boat.

Luckily, with the wind astern of us, the voyage back to Leith took no time at all, although we were nearly out of coal when we arrived and Mr. Kemp was quite fatigued, what with pulling all the levers and other fiddly things, keeping the furnace bright and looking after all the survivors that he had brought on board. I just played the dutiful handfasted wife and obeyed orders. At times I was tempted to tug my wet forelock and say: "Aye, aye, sir" but I refrained and stuck to my task of steering and getting wet.

There were five survivors, all waterlogged and bedraggled but alive. The most important of them was Louise, of course looking sheepish and forlorn, but very glad to be rescued from the grasp of the French officer, who had proved to be much less than a gentleman once he had got what he wanted, which was a free passage to France. There was the American owner of the vessel, who was Louise's mysterious friend and a notable landowner and merchant in his home country. There was the Frenchman himself, now safely back in custody, and an anonymous but quite handsome seaman named Joe. He hailed from Baltimore; he was very tall and muscular and helped willingly with the steering, much to my relief. I had hoped that Mr. Kemp would be jealous of the attention Joe paid me, but he seemed quite unconscious of the man from Baltimore. Perhaps the fact that Joe was married helped.

It was only when we arrived back that my adventures began to make sense, and my life took the twists that led to me being here, and my picture sitting on the wall. But don't let me rush, for that might spoil everything and you deserve to have it unfold as I did, piece by piece. Once you have heard the whole thing, then you will understand why I think that Willie Kemp was the worst, most black-hearted schemer alive, damn him for the most handsome and amiable villain I have ever met.

A translucent pink dawn was already easing over the Forth and spreading tentacles of greyish light on to the dark buildings of Leith as we chugged dirtily in. By then I was the most appalling mess, with soot smuts all over me, my hair a fright and my clothes just a sodden shambles, but I was awake and I was truly alive for I had been useful and achieved what I had intended, which is always a good feeling. The first thing I noted was the crowd that waited for us on the Shore. I had thought that Aunt Elspeth might have been there, but she had brought the whole clan with her, and scores of people that I did not know, as well as some familiar faces. I must admit to some trepidation, for however successful we had been, I had yet to face Aunt Elspeth about my week's absence and I had not forgotten her previous threats of birchings and the like. I felt certain parts of me quiver and hoped attention would be diverted to Louise.

"How did the news spread?" I wondered, but Mr. Kemp merely smiled.

"News of a ship wreck always travels fast."

I steered *Mary* alongside the Shore and a score of willing hands were ready with ropes and help for the survivors. It was then that fatigue gripped me and I sagged at the wheel and felt my head swirl. I did not swoon though. Some inner strength kept me upright. You remember that my dears; however weak and tired you may be, there are always some reserves of strength within you when they are needed.

"William!" Mrs. Cairnsmuir was first to greet us, clasping Mr. Kemp in both arms and embracing him, with no regard to his soaking wet clothes or the coal dust that smeared him from head to boots. I was shocked at the impropriety of her behaviour to a mere mechanic, and more than a little jealous, for that should have been me holding him so close.

Aunt Elspeth hurried to Louise, who had managed to drag herself to her feet and was trying to make sense of the blonde shambles on top of her head. She looked up as her mother approached and stood slightly shamefaced.

Aunt Elspeth touched her lightly on the shoulder but there was no doubting the mingled anger and relief in her voice. "Now you've had your little adventure, girlie, have you found even a modicum of sense?"

Louise nodded emphatically and Aunt Elspeth pulled her into a tight hug that lasted for a good two minutes as they sobbed together as only two women can.

I released my grip on the wooden spokes of the wheel and stepped unsteadily onto the Shore. I stood alone, wondering how I had survived and where I should go and what I should do while Lieutenant John Forres, looking surprisingly efficient and quite dapper in those splendid white breeches, ordered a detachment of his regiment to take control of the French prisoner. He smiled and bowed to me, and I curtseyed back, quite taken with this new side of him. Perhaps, I thought, perhaps there was something behind the dandy appearance, but I killed that thought, for he would certainly not want to know me now, after my misadventures with Willie Kemp.

I knew I was beyond the pale of respectable society. I had pushed myself into a dark corner and there I would stay. I continued to stand alone while seemingly half the gentlefolk of Edinburgh fussed around Mr. Kemp and Louise, and the rugged and handsome Joe winked at me.

"You did well," he said and held out his hand. "Thank you for saving my life."

I took his hand, which was hard and horny and honest. "It was a great pleasure," I lied, and then I burst into tears once more.

It may have been reaction after the excitement, or possibly sheer exhaustion, but whatever the reason, I sank to the ground, trembling. The American seaman and ship-owner were crouched down at my side speaking with those lovely transatlantic accents Willie Kemp arrived.

"Miss Lamont! Alison?" There was genuine concern in his voice as he stood over me. "My God, are you hurt?" I saw him tower above me, head and shoulders taller than everybody in that heterogeneous crowd, and I heard him shout.

"Bring a coach! Quickly!"

I was no longer surprised that people rushed to obey Mr. Kemp, but I was astonished when he lifted me in those strong arms and placed me on one seat of Mrs. Cairnsmuir's own carriage. I lay there, dazed, admiring the coat of arms on the panel above Mr. Kemp's head and wondering where I had seen that device of a crown and crossed swords before. I did not care, especially not when Mr. Kemp leant over me and kissed me as gently as I have ever been kissed in my life.

"It's all right now," he said. "Everything will be all right now." Then he smiled and everything in the world was golden. "Let's get those wet clothes off you and get you into something dry."

I tried to protest, to say that it was hardly decent, but he only laughed. "I've seen you before, remember, and anyway, last night was our wedding night."

Last night? That handfasting ceremony seemed a year ago and a million miles away. I stared at him as through a long dark tunnel but before I knew it he had slipped dry things on me, although I have no idea from where they came, and when I woke he was carrying me, huddled in a coach blanket, right through the front door of Cairnsmuir House.

"We can't come here," I said, more than slightly dazed. "Mrs. Cairnsmuir won't like it. Take me to our cottage in the hills."

"Mrs. Cairnsmuir will be pleased to have you," Mr. Kemp told me, smiling softly.

I looked around, seeing Mrs. Cairnsmuir herself, with Aunt Elspeth by her side and Louise with dark shadows around her eyes and her shoulders drooping. I braced myself for a torrent of accusation and abuse, but instead, all I saw was concern.

"You sleep easy, Miss Lamont," Mrs. Cairnsmuir said softly. "You're safe now."

"I'm always safe with Willie Kemp," I told her. "He's a real gentleman." I dropped my voice to a whisper as I boasted of the man that I loved. "Do you know that he walked in on me naked and did not take any advantage at all?"

Mrs. Cairnsmuir shook her head. "I did not hear that," but her face seemed to float away as Mr. Kemp carried me into the largest and softest bed that I have ever seen.

"I must leave you now," he was smiling but I clung to his neck, protesting that he could not leave me alone again. "It's only for a short while," he said and prised free my hands.

The door closed softly but a trio of maids, supervised by Aunt Elspeth, were there to ease me out of my clothes and into a silk nightgown that floated over me, caressing all my curves. There were silk sheets too, and a pillow so soft that it seemed ethereal, and then I was dreaming, with a host of images of the past two weeks cascading through my mind so I moaned and twisted and called for Willie Kemp.

"I'm here," he said, and he was, sitting by my bed with his hand on mine. "I'll always be here."

Or was that a dream?

I remembered, then, where I had seen that device of a crown and crossed swords that had decorated the coach. The same symbols had been on the cutlery in Willie Kemp's hut. "You are a thief," I told him, as I drifted away again. "You stole from Cairnsmuir House." But Willie Kemp did not look in the least abashed as he smiled at me, and gently tucked me in.

When I awoke again it was full daylight and there was a warm fire in the grate. Mr. Kemp was dozing in his chair but he jerked awake when I softly called his name.

"Mr. Kemp?" I could feel the soot from *Mary* combating the salt to scrape the lining of my throat.

"Alison? Miss Lamont?"

I nodded, luxuriating in the comfortable warmth of that splendid room. "I am pleased to see you there, Mr. Kemp." I reached for him, but he stood a finger's length out of reach.

Mr. Kemp looked as uncomfortable as I had ever seen him. "Miss Lamont. There are things that you should know about me."

I smiled, for, as I have already said, I was very young and still naïve, but I was about to learn the duplicity of that man that I trusted more than anybody else on earth. The scheming Willie Kemp!

"I know enough," I stopped his words by half rising from the bed and pressing a finger to his lips. "I know that I love you and that we are handfasted."

He removed my finger; rather roughly, I thought and eased me back under the covers. The touch of his hands thrilled me. "There are other people involved, Miss Lamont, so things are not quite as simple as you would wish."

"I only wish you," I said.

Mr. Kemp sighed, shook his head and gave me the saddest of all smiles. He rose abruptly and left the room, reappearing a few minutes later with a whole host at his tail. There was Aunt Elspeth, and Louise of course, you could never keep her away from anything with even a hint of scandal. Then there was Mrs. Cairnsmuir with her severe face. When I wondered what she thought about me soiling her best silk sheets I shrugged, and cried a little, and then forgot about her as I looked at the rest of the company. There was that auburn haired woman who I had met once before, when she stood with her back to the wall, saying nothing; and there was John Forres, once more the dandy, but now I had seen the man behind the facade and all was not as it was. He looked at me and smiled, and I smiled back, quite ready to forgive him any perceived transgressions.

"Good evening," I said to the assembled company and tried to curtsey from my bed. I failed and succeeded only in unsettling myself as my pillow slid to the floor. Mr. Kemp and John Forres both made a lunge to rescue it, collided before they reached my bed and glared at each other for a second until Mrs. Cairnsmuir said a single short word that separated them.

After that little incident, they all clustered around, some standing, some smiling and the more impertinent even sitting on my bed. Louise came closer and pretended to be concerned about my welfare even as she looked sidelong into the dressing table mirror to admire her profile.

"As this is my house," Mrs. Cairnsmuir said to me, "I shall speak first and you shall listen."

I nodded meekly. What else could I do? I saw my aunt's grim face and wondered once more what penalties she would inflict upon me. "Yes Mrs. Cairnsmuir," I said.

"For a start, you can drop that pretence at timidity, Miss Lamont. It takes a strong woman to live alone in a cottage in the wilds, and a strong woman to steer a boat in a Forth squall. There is a time and place for pretence and a time and place for truth, and this is the latter. Do you understand?"

I felt myself colouring up to the roots of my tangled black hair. "Of course," I retorted, quite sharply. "I do not tell lies, Mrs. Cairnsmuir!"

"That's better! There has been enough play- acting here, and it will stop right now." Her tone moderated a little so it was less like a file and more like a cheese grater. "I believe that you know all these people present?"

I ran my eyes over them again. You have no idea how vulnerable you can feel lying in an unfamiliar bed when a collection of relatives and strangers are staring down at you. Especially when you feel as guilty as I did. "I know everybody except the lady with red hair."

"I thought not." Mrs. Cairnsmuir said firmly. "That is Elizabeth Kemp."

I might have given a small scream. I certainly felt faint as I looked at the tall, handsome and eminently capable looking Elizabeth Kemp. She looked back at me, faintly amused, and I wondered if she was about to launch some attack on my person, or was just enjoying my humiliation. I closed my eyes to hide the sudden tears as everything began to make sense.

Of course, Mr. Kemp was married; he was tall, handsome and always knew just what to say to a woman. Who else but a married man would know that? And that explained his long absence while I was in the cottage; he was with his wife, where he ought to be. It also explained why he had not wished to marry me; he could not if he already had a wife.

"I am pleased to make your acquaintance, Miss Lamont," Elizabeth Kemp was mocking me now, holding out her hand in pretence at friendship while she hid her distaste behind that false smile. She was shapely too, taller than me and with a nice figure behind those flimsy clothes. She did not have my plumpness but had that correct proportion of curves and swells that men seem to prefer above all other womanly shape. I hated her all the more. "William has told me all about you."

"What?" I stared at her, and swivelled my eyes to her blackguard, deceiving husband. "He told you about me?"

"Of course he did." The wronged wife's laughter was as appealing as everything else about her. I felt terribly, frustratingly and pointlessly jealous. "He always tells me about his doings."

He would, I reasoned. He was a gentleman in every respect. Suddenly I remembered his politeness but the lack of shock, or passion, when he saw me naked. There was small wonder at that now; he had probably seen the curvaceous Elizabeth naked a thousand times; indeed he had probably just come from their marriage bed. I wondered, savagely, if he had shared that experience with the lovely Elizabeth as well.

I took her hand of course. Mother always emphasised that one must always appear polite, even when one is filled with hatred and fear and bitter, bitter disappointment. John Forres was watching, smiling and nodding. He would make some woman a fine catch.

"So now you do know everybody." Mrs. Cairnsmuir said. "And it is time for explanations."

I nodded. How could I explain that I loved this woman's husband, or that I had run away from home to be with a married man? I swallowed. "What do you want me to say?"

Mrs. Cairnsmuir smiled. "Oh, we don't want you to say anything, Miss Lamont. We know everything there is to know about you. William does not keep us in the dark." I was surprised when she showed a little hesitation. "Or should I say, I thought he told us all, but he had not mentioned that small episode in the cottage that you just revealed to me."

I blushed anew as I recalled telling Mrs. Cairnsmuir about Mr. Kemp finding me naked. I cursed my wayward mouth.

"What was that?" Elizabeth Kemp arched her eyebrows in enquiry "If it concerns William, then I must know about it."

"Not this time, Elizabeth," Mr. Kemp said, firmly, and I knew that there were some things my Willie Kemp did not share. I thanked him with my eyes, even as I wished the bed would sink into the floor, taking me with it.

"No, Miss Lamont, it is we who owe you an explanation. Is that not right, William Kemp?" Mrs. Cairnsmuir looked sternly at Mr. Kemp, who had the decency to look humble, if not subdued.

"Yes, mother."

It took me a small while to register what Mr. Kemp had said, but to judge by the silence in the room, everybody else already knew. "Mother?" I repeated in a voice so soft that even I barely heard it.

"Indeed." Willie Kemp knelt down beside the bed and rested his elbows a few inches from my head. "Mrs. Cairnsmuir is my mother. My full name is William Kemp Cairnsmuir."

I do not think that I have ever been more surprised, or humbled, in my life. "But you are a mechanic, an artisan. You are..." I stopped as the full implications hit me. Mr. Kemp had never pretended to be anything but a humble mechanic, but on the other hand, he had never denied that he was a gentleman and a landowner, because I had never asked him. I had merely assumed that he was what he appeared to be. In fact, I had judged by appearances and those few moments of casual conversation when Louise had made such disparaging comments about Mr. Kemp and his steamboat.

"I am William Kemp Cairnsmuir," Mr. Kemp told me. "My other title, which I rarely use, is the Earl of Cairnsmuir."

"Oh my goodness." Rather than Mr. Kemp being of a lower social status than me, it was I who was far lower down the scale. But that hardly mattered as he was married to Elizabeth. I paused for a second. Elizabeth Kemp? If William was surnamed Cairnsmuir, then why had she not taken his name? Perhaps Kemp was the family name and Cairnsmuir merely the title: I always found these things confusing.

"Indeed," Mr. Kemp said. "You are handfasted to the Earl of Cairnsmuir."

"But why?" I asked, completely at a loss. "If you are married to Elizabeth, why play this silly little game with me?" Although I lay in bed in his house, my temper rose at the thought that the Earl of Cairnsmuir had been playing tricks on me all this time. I have a wicked temper, my dears, as you all have had cause to find out. That day I unleashed it on Willie Kemp and I did not hold back my vicious tongue, finishing, some moments later, with: "You are not a gentleman, Mr. Kemp, or Mr. Cairnsmuir or whatever name you choose to adopt!"

"I am certainly not married to Elizabeth," Mr. Kemp had survived my onslaught with patience and tolerance; now he seemed vastly amused. "Whatever made you think that?"

"Your mother made me think that," I pointed out, by now completely roused and ready to battle with Earls, Mrs. Cairnsmuirs or the devil himself. Perhaps that was an example of my wild Highland ways, but I could no more deny myself the distinct pleasure of shouting at this man that I loved dearly, but could no longer have. "Mrs. Cairnsmuir introduced her as Elizabeth Kemp."

It was Elizabeth herself who leant forward and placed a capable hand on my shoulder. "I am Elizabeth Kemp," she agreed quietly, and with all her husband's humour in her equally brown eyes. "Elizabeth Kemp Cairnsmuir. The Kemp part is our mother's maiden name. We are brother and sister, you see."

I saw. And once again I began to cry, more in frustration than in anything else. "So what is happening?"

"Perhaps I had better explain," Aunt Elspeth said, and everybody else in the room stepped back except for Willie Kemp.

"You were sent here to find a suitable husband." Aunt Elspeth began, "and I really believed that John Forres would be the answer. He is a handsome, eligible man and with him, you would have no financial worries. Nor would you be worried about any faithlessness, for he has no real interest in women."

I nodded. I understood so far. John Forrest took a punch of snuff and nodded in complete amiability

"But that night of the riot, you also met Cairnsmuir – Willie Kemp - and things became more complicated." Aunt Elspeth raised her eyebrows to Mr. Kemp, who gave a nearly imperceptible nod, as if of agreement. "You see, that night that you lay in his bed, Earl Cairnsmuir came here and told me that he had already fallen in love with you."

I looked at Mr. Kemp, who grinned. I resolved to have further hot words with that man later when there were no witnesses. "By why all the pretence, then?" I demanded. By now I was far too cross with the scheming devil to care about our relative social positions.

"Let me continue," Aunt Elspeth was smiling. "You must understand that there is a difference in social standing, and the Earl of Cairnsmuir had to be certain that you were the right woman for him."

"Oh, is that so?" I glanced over to Mr. Kemp with my temper rising by the minute. If he thought he had heard the worst of me he was about to be made aware of his mistake. I felt the words building up within me ready to launch themselves with hooked and poisoned claws at the ego and person of that most devious of handsome men that I loved to distraction.

"It was not William's idea, but my orders," Lady Cairnsmuir said slowly. "He would have proposed that very night, but I insisted that he test you first."

"Did you indeed! You had him test me, did you? And he agreed to this charade?" I spoke as coldly as I could, although my anger was hotter than the devil's furnace on Halloween.

Aunt Elspeth continued. "John Forres had also expressed his interest in you, so we decided to press his suit and see if you would be swayed by money and lands, for, as far as you were concerned, Willie Kemp was only a mechanic."

My temper did not diminish one whit. "Indeed." I glared at Mr. Kemp, resolved to speak more fully on this subject later. I was certain he would receive the roughest edge of my tongue. He had not yet properly met my wild Highland ways.

"You, however, remained true," Aunt Elspeth said, quietly.

"If you will remember, I examined you quite thoroughly during your second visit to the Forres Residence." Mrs. Cairnsmuir said.

"I remember that very well, Madam." My temper was as hot as ever. I must have glared at everybody there, reserving my most poisonous eyes for Mr. Kemp-Cairnsmuir, the devious blackguard that I was ever more resolved to scold most thoroughly as soon as we were alone together and I could enjoy the experience.

"But, however much you sounded sincere, I needed more proof, for I hold William Kemp very dear." Mrs. Cairnsmuir continued. "Of course, he kept us all fully informed of all your plans and schemes."

"Of course," I said again. My future conversation with Mr. Kemp took on yet another element. I did not think that he would enjoy it in the slightest. My palm itched to slap his face or perhaps some other more prominent part of his person.

"So he found a suitable cottage where you would be safe but where you could experience some of the hardships you might find as a mechanic's wife."

I nodded but said nothing, remembering the loneliness and the cold.

"You understand why, of course? If you remained staunch in difficult circumstances, you would probably remain staunch in the good times." Mrs. Cairnsmuir smiled faintly. "You know the old saying, when poverty comes in the door, love flies out the window? Well, we were ensuring that love would remain."

"So you left me alone in the hills for a week?" There was no pretence in the chill warning in my voice.

"You were never alone," Mrs. Cairnsmuir gave a small smile. "William was watching you all the time."

I remembered that shadowy figure in the mist, and the footprints in the snow. Both would have been Willie Kemp. My temper cooled a little, but only a little. As the poet said, I nursed my wrath to keep it warm.

"And the final ordeal," Mrs. Cairnsmuir was solemn faced. "Would you agree to a trial marriage, the handfast? You did, although at no time did my son say that he loved you."

"He was testing my commitment all the time?" I decided not to have that long conversation with Mr. Kemp. I remembered the humiliation of Mother Faa's probing and decided on quite another course of action.

"I was," Mr. Kemp confirmed. "And you passed every time."

"Indeed," I said, with my temper now in control of my better judgement. Now take some advice from an old woman, girls, we all have a temper, it is in our blood, but the trick is to control it. If you learn to direct your temper, you can use it, but if it controls you, then you are in danger of losing everything. Listen and learn. I learned the hard way, with some advice from a very wise friend of mine.

"And now, Miss Lamont," Mr. Kemp struggled to get down on one knee. That may sound a strange thing to say, but in my days breeches could be so tight it was impossible for men to bend. It did make for some splendid views for us ladies but could be awkward at times. "I can honestly ask you to be my wife. And I mean my real wife, this time and not a temporary handfasted arrangement."

I felt the atmosphere in that room tighten as everybody waited for my assent. Even Louise was quiet, watching me through dark eyes.

"Could we be alone, please?" I asked. "This is an important moment in a woman's life and I must take the time to discuss things fully."

There was a slight sigh of disappointment but everybody left quietly, one at a time. Elizabeth Kemp was last as she paused to smile encouragingly from the door. Her brother waved her away and waited expectantly by my bed.

My slap took Mr. Kemp quite by surprise, catching him on the left side of his face and nearly toppling him from his knees. As he stared at me in disbelief, I fought the urge to follow with a second. "Now Mr. Kemp," I said. "Now I will agree to marry you, but if you ever treat me like that again…"

I never did finish that sentence, for Mr. Kemp's mouth was on mine, and his hands were pulling me close. So you see, if I had allowed my temper to control me and had landed another slap, I might never have gained that kiss, or Willie Kemp as my husband for over fifty years.

So remember my dears: a good man is worth taking trouble over, but you are also important in your own selves. You might well meet a man as tricky and devious and downright treacherous as Willie Kemp, but if you thole the hardships, the rewards can also be good.

So now you know all.

0840

66454472R00095

Made in the USA
San Bernardino, CA
12 January 2018